ABOVE HIGH TIDE

BLAIR POLLY

D1719242

ISBN-13: 978-1484096376
ISBN-10: 1484096371

Please note: This is a work of fiction.
Although many of the places described in this book are real, the
characters and businesses portrayed here are fictional.

DEDICATION

For my friends, family, and jade hunters everywhere.

ACKNOWLEDGMENTS

Thanks to Deb Potter, Barbara Polly, Marie Nordstrand, Leslie McQueen, and the many others who have given me encouragement and help during the writing of this book. Also a big thanks to NaNoWriMo for getting me started on this book in November of 2012.

Chapter 1 - Thursday Afternoon

The dog came at him from nowhere. He flinched, raising an arm, but didn't have time to brace himself before the impact smashed him off his feet. As he hit the ground, the gun clattered from his hand and the wind exploded from his lungs.

Gasping for breath under a growling mountain of fur, he bucked and twisted. The more he fought, the deeper the dog's sharp canines dug into his flesh. A searing pain flashed up his arm from wrist to shoulder.

"Arrrrgh! Get off me!"

At first he didn't recognise the scream as his own, but a burst of adrenalin cleared his mind, allowing him to focus. He saw his contorted expression reflected in the animal's eyes only inches from his face. A low rumble vibrated deep in the dog's throat.

As he struggled, his free arm flailed around searching for a weapon, anything that might help him stop the animal tearing at his flesh. When he found a lump of quartz, he clutched it tight, hoping it would prove his salvation.

But before he could swing the rock towards the dog's massive head, a boot stepped on his wrist, pinning it to the ground.

"I wouldn't hit my dog with that rock mister. Not if you want to keep your arm."

Chapter 2 - Monday Morning

The turn of the century workingman's cottage was typical of its era. Only a room and a hallway wide, it ran four rooms deep. A narrow section at the back contained a brick-paved patio, lemon tree, small vegetable garden, and the remnants of an old shed Sam planned to turn into a sauna when he got around to it.

From the deck, the picture-postcard view always astounded him. Far below lay Wellington city, a crescent of skyscrapers sweeping around the edge of its clear blue harbour. Bush-clad hills dotted with red, green, and silver roofs, surrounded the city's compact centre.

On the far side of the harbour, a haze-filled Hutt Valley stretched off into the distance, rising in elevation towards the Rimutaka Ranges to the east, and the Tararua's to the north.

Sam never tired of this spot. The house itself may not be worth much, but he never tired of the panorama laid out before him.

He'd moved in just after his divorce three years previously. His half of the proceeds from selling the family home meant this tiny cottage was all he could afford at the time. Now he realised it was all he needed. If anything, he preferred the casual living the cottage provided over the formality of the much swankier place he and his ex had once owned.

He was pleased he no longer had to worry about getting finger-marks on the pristine white walls or scratches in the imported timber flooring. Life in the house he and his ex-wife had built had been like living in an art gallery, characterless and sterile, and not to Sam's taste at all.

His old cottage was relaxed in its history. Its leaded windows were slumped and bowed with time, and the rusticated matai floorboards were flawed, but both wore their age and scars with a grace that the modern materials in his previous house could never do.

Wide rimu skirting boards and timber work throughout the

interior, gave the cottage character. Rich colours on the walls, gave the cottage warmth, making him feel at ease in surroundings that fit him like an old pair of slippers, slightly battered yet comfortable and snug.

Sam had steady work when he wanted it. Not that work ranked high on his list of priorities. There were lots of things he found more absorbing than looking for runaway teenagers, gathering evidence against a cheating spouse, or tracking down stolen property through his extensive network of contacts. Even working with the new technologies that had started to play a bigger part in his business, and dealing with problems such as identity theft and electronic fraud, couldn't hold his attention for long. Rarely would a month go by, before he felt the need to get out of town for a while.

He worked out of a small room above his garage. There was no receptionist, no plush carpeting, no flash espresso machine, or executive bathroom. Not that he would have wanted them anyway. None of that stuff impressed him. Besides, he was out so much of the time, spending big bucks for somewhere to keep his desk, a couple of arm chairs, a bookcase, and a bank of storage cupboards seemed pointless. Plush the place may not be, but it was comfortable, like a bookworm's study, or the back room in a museum somewhere, and that suited him just fine.

Work related material from the cases he'd investigated, only filled one cupboard in his office. The other five were filled with articles relating to his interests, and his collections. The best pieces of his collection he kept in a glass-fronted display case pushed against one wall.

Sometimes, after a good payday, when he didn't have another job on, he'd play poker at one of the casinos. At other times, especially when the weather was good, he'd travel around the country panning for gold, fossicking for minerals and gemstones, or searching for fossils, and early Māori, or European, artefacts.

Poker was a family tradition, taught to him by his father. Sam often thought of his old man when he played. He remembered the times they spent together as he was growing up, and the long talks they'd had. He'd learned a lot about tactics, discipline, and reading people's body language during those sessions. He'd also learned to trust his gut and calculate odds. Sometimes his father would set him a mathematical puzzle to work out as they played.

"You've got to be able to work out the odds quickly, Sammy," his father would say. "Then you've got time to study your opponent's behaviour."

But, despite enjoying poker, and being pretty good at it after all the expert tuition, playing cards was an indoor activity, and Sam true love was being in the great outdoors.

His real passion, was hunting for precious stones, fossils and artefacts. Ever since he found his first piece of jade, a teardrop shaped pebble, poking out of a shingle bank on the West Coast beach he and his university geology class had been searching, he'd been hooked. Since then, nothing got his blood racing quite like a treasure hunt.

Now days, he went fossicking whenever he had the chance. Not just because it gave him an excuse to travel out into the countryside, but because every time he walked down a beach or up a river, he had the chance of finding the next item for his collection. Every step he took while looking for jade, artefacts, garnets, serpentine, or ambergris, brought him that much closer to that next piece of treasure, and the rush of adrenalin that accompanied the moment of discovery.

His cupboards were full of treasure. Not treasure in the traditional sense. Not the gold pieces-of-eight, or the emerald filled chests one might find in pirate stories, but treasures none the less, treasures of history, of nature, treasures rare, beautiful, and valued by the societies that interwove them into their culture. They were also items that held extra significance to him because of the journeys he'd taken to discover them.

His most recent find, sat in pride of place on the edge of his desk, doing duty as a paperweight. The fossilised shells were light in colour, and cast in superb detail. They had, at one time, been buried on an ancient seabed. Over millions of years, minerals had replaced the organic material and turned the shells into the rocky clump of limestone that sat before him.

The fossil wasn't particularly valuable, except maybe to Sam and the odd palaeontologist. Still it gave him the warm fuzzies whenever he looked at it.

He'd found the piece on his last trip to the South Island in the Nelson area, an hour's walk up a creek in the Wairoa Gorge. From what he'd read about similar fossils uncovered in the area, the shells were from the Triassic period over 400 million years ago, and among the oldest ever found in New Zealand.

Whenever his 41 years were getting him down, he would look at the fist-sized rock and see things in a different perspective, see how young he really was in the overall scheme of things.

It was hard to comprehend a million years let alone 400 million, even harder to imagine how the earth had changed over that time, the species of animals that had come and gone, the ice ages, the rise and falls in sea levels, continents moving. Thinking about such things made him feel insignificant, but it also made him determined to make the most of the time he had, and not waste his life by working too much. There were too many interesting things out there to learn and uncover, too many artefacts and semi-precious stones for him to find.

As he sat at his desk drinking his morning coffee and pondering the questions of life, the universe, and everything, the phone rang.

"Sam McKee, how can I help?"

"I believe you retrieve stolen property," the voice on the other end said. "Some prick's stolen a Mercedes belonging to me."

"Have you tried the police?"

"I don't want the police involved. A driver I use in Auckland occasionally, Jimmy Sands, you know, big guy, not afraid of a bit of rough and tumble when required. He told me you were discrete."

Sam remembered his last encounter with Jimmy on a

recovery job a few years back. He'd not been very impressed. Jimmy's indiscriminate use of violence meant that he'd had to distance himself from the job to avoid arrest. Jimmy hadn't been so clever.

"Yeah, I know Jimmy. Is he out of jail?"

"Jimmy's a good boy now. Well, most of the time anyway."

"This job legit?" Sam asked.

"I own the car if that's what you mean. Are you interested? I'll make it worth your while."

"Give me your name and number. I'll see if I can clear space in my schedule and ring you back in an hour or so."

After making a note of Trevor Graeme's details, Sam called Jimmy's cell.

"Sand's Limousine Services."

"Hiya Jimmy. It's Sam, Sam McKee."

"Sam. I've been expecting a call from you. Mr G got in touch then?"

"Just a few minutes ago. What's his story?"

"He's just a guy trying to make a buck. A businessman, you know. Might be a bit on the shady side at times, but who's a hundred percent kosher right?"

"Am I likely to get arrested or shot working for him?"

"Nah, I work for him all the time. He pays good too."

After chatting with Jimmy a while, Sam hung up, leaned back in his chair, and considered what he'd heard. His gut told him not to trust Jimmy's judgement, so he made another call, this time to an old friend of his father's. One who had been around the Wellington scene since the early days.

Rodney was no saint, but despite having done a couple stints in prison, there were few men Sam trusted more. More importantly, his father had trusted Rodney's judgement, and that spoke volumes.

"So what's Mr G want you to do, wack somebody?" Rodney cackled down the phone line, his laugh harsh from the forty a day he smoked.

"Very funny ... no he wants me to find a missing car. No cops, which sounds a bit dodgy. Do you know much about him?"

"He's just your typical bad boy turned businessman really, does a bit of this and that. He'll probably tell you he's a property developer, but in reality most of his money comes from his brothels. He's got two in Auckland, one in Wellington, and another in Christchurch, if I remember correctly."

"Am I likely to get any surprises working for him?"

"Hey, it's your call Sammy boy. All I can say is, if you do find this car of his, make sure there isn't a body in the boot before you drive it anywhere. Mr G has a tendency to get angry when things don't go his way, if you know what I mean."

"Okay mate, thanks for the heads-up."

"Be careful Sammy, this guy may look like he's on the level, but I assure you, he's got no scruples, no integrity. Not like when your dad was around."

After disconnecting the call, Sam was undecided about whether to take the job or not. He didn't really like the sound of this Mr G guy. The turning point in his decision making process came when he logged on to his online banking and checked his current account balances.

When he saw the numbers, he realised he'd been having a little too much time off recently.

Despite his reservations, Sam decided to risk it. This was a chance to make some fast money, just what he needed to top his funds up. If he didn't like what he saw when he found the car, he'd walk away.

Sam picked up the phone. When Mr G answered, Sam put on his poker voice, unemotional and direct. "Before I take on the job, I have two questions."

"What?"

"How much are you willing to pay, and when I find the car, can I handle the retrieval so nobody gets hurt?"

"So nobody gets hurt? What makes you say that?"

"Look, I don't need to be Albert Einstein to figure out you've got an agenda here. Believe me I don't care about your business. I just don't want anyone to get hurt because of information I provide." Sam always did research on his clients, and it amused him when a prospective client was shocked by his knowledge of them. "So, do you still want me to find your car?"

"Look pal, all I want is my Merc back. I'll pay you fifteen percent of the car's value. That's almost 20k, tax free. Just don't involve the cops, and don't ask questions about things that don't concern you. Got it?"

The deal sounded too good to pass up, providing he found the car that is. If not, he'd get nothing.

"It's your money Mr Graeme."

*****

Brutus ate from a large stainless steel bowl on the floor. Every morning he got a slab of dog roll and a handful of biscuits. His master had taught him to sit before he ate. Only after he'd been given the correct command, was he allowed to touch his food.

Brutus looked up at the man. A drop of saliva fell from his jaws as he sat, eager to eat. When the bowl hit the linoleum, it took all of the dog's willpower not to lurch forward.

Ten seconds later, the man spoke. "Ok boy, chow down."

As Brutus devoured his food, the man sat down at the kitchen table and pulled a photo of a young girl out of his pocket. He stared at it while he finished his cup of tea, his eyes never leaving the girl's face.

"Pretty young thing isn't she Brutus?" the man said as he stood to put his cup in the sink, sliding the photo back into his top pocket.

Brutus turned his head towards the man when he spoke, then scoffed the last of his dog biscuits, knowing they'd be leaving soon. It was the same every day. Food first, and then he'd be put in the wire cage on the back of his master's truck.

Chapter 3 - Two Weeks Later

It took Sam time, but eventually he traced Mr G's stolen Mercedes to a car importer in the Hutt Valley. The firm, it seemed, had trade going both ways across the Pacific. Cheap imports from Japan came into New Zealand, and luxury cars of dubious provenance were shipped back the other way.

Curious as to why Mr G had been so insistent the police were not involved, Sam's active imagination had come up with a hundred possibilities, not that he was ever likely to know the whole story for sure.

What could be the problem? If Mr G owned the car, the only thing he could think of was that there must be something in the car he didn't want the cops to find. Were drugs involved? Guns? Stolen property maybe?

He told himself not to worry about it. There was no point wasting time guessing. As long he got paid the agreed price when he got the car back, and didn't get arrested in the process, Sam could live with a little mystery.

It wouldn't be the first time he'd been curious while on the job. Repossession and recovery were Sam's specialities. It was amazing the things people wanted him to recover. He'd recovered everything from CD's containing intimate personal photos, to a laptop computer with a PhD candidate's thesis on it. He'd found family heirlooms, runaway brides, and stolen art. He had contacts all over the country, some less reputable than others.

Sam greased the wheels to keep information flowing. He never failed to reward those whose information helped him get a result. But sometimes info wasn't easy to come by, despite the number of people you knew, or what you were prepared to pay for it.

After a week of contacting anyone who might give him a lead on the missing Mercedes, he'd turned up nothing. Then, just as he was starting to run out of ideas, he met a bloke he knew in an early opening pub down by the railway station.

After buying the mechanic a few drinks, and questioning him about any dodgy operations he knew about, the mechanic mentioned a Hutt Valley importer he did some under-the-table work for on occasion.

What the mechanic really needed was a life membership to Alcoholics Anonymous and a lesson in discretion. Instead, Sam bought him the bottle of scotch he demanded in exchange for the firm's name, with a promise of another if the tip paid off.

After driving to the Hutt Valley, Sam managed to confirm the importer had the Mercedes hidden behind a van in the rear of their warehouse by pretending to be a customer wanting to upgrade his Toyota Surf and sneaking a look around while pretending to use the loo.

The rest of the job was easy. That night, he bypassed the importer's cheap unmonitored alarm system, and used bolt cutters on the padlock securing the gate.

Sam often found that thieves had the worst security. Maybe it was laziness. Maybe they assumed that because they were criminals, everyone else must be honest. In either case, it made his work easier.

Once inside the premises Sam gave the Mercedes a quick once over, hoping to discover what all the drama was about. He checked the boot, under the spare tire, under the front seats, and in the glove box. He even got down on his hands and knees and pointed his torch at the underside of the vehicle to see if something had been wired to the chassis, but found nothing out of the ordinary.

The item or items Mr G wanted back, were either well hidden, or had already been removed by the thieves. In either case, he wasn't worried. His job was to return the car, the rest was Mr G's problem. As least the boot wasn't full of drugs, a dead body, or something else that could get him arrested were he unlucky enough to get stopped and searched by the cops on his way to the drop-off point.

As he drove back to town, Sam took special care to keep his speed under the limit. Regardless of how clean it looked, getting stopped by the cops and having his name forever linked with the car in a police database somewhere was not his idea of working smart. Who knew what Mr G might use the car for in future.

Sam had just started to enjoy driving the luxury automobile when flashing lights and the sound of a siren raced up behind him. His heart leapt into his throat. Holding his breath, he eased his foot off the accelerator and started pulling towards the shoulder, his eye frantically searching the rear vision mirror for the source of the noise.

When an ambulance screamed by, he shook his fist at the lights disappearing into the distance. "Don't do that to me. You'll give me a heart attack!"

After his fright, the rest of the drop went to plan. He parked the Mercedes at the pre-arranged spot, wiped his prints off the car, and walked to the main road two blocks away where he phoned Mr G to advise him of his success.

"Well done Sam. Swing by my office tomorrow morning and I'll sort you out."

*****

Sam awoke refreshed after sleeping well for the first time in weeks. The missing car had niggled at his mind for the last fortnight, but with the conclusion of the case, that anxiety had disappeared. Instead he'd dreamed of empty beaches and greenstone.

It was a sunny day, so after having a quick breakfast, he decided to walk through the greenbelt into town to collect his cash. It would only take him half an hour, and besides, he could do with the exercise.

Mr Graeme's office was in a building on Manners Street. When he reached Graeme Developments sixth floor suite, he paused at the open door.

Behind a desk in the outer office sat a woman in her early thirties. She had the phone pressed to the side of her head and appeared to be in robust discussion with someone on the other end of the line. When she noticed Sam in the doorway, she lifted her head, giving him a nod of acknowledgement, pushed a wisp of hair behind her ear, and continued her conversation.

"I don't care what you say, I'm not authorising this invoice until you supply me with a breakdown of costs."

Her stunning green eyes made Sam happy to wait. He lingered a few metres away, out of her direct line of sight, so he could observe her without her noticing he was staring.

When she hung up the phone, Sam approached her desk.

"Can I help you?" she asked.

He beamed a smile in her direction. "Hi, I'm Sam McKee. I'm here to see Mr Graeme."

Lydia couldn't help smiling back. Sam's eyes were a beautiful pale blue that matched his cotton shirt. His gaze seemed to bore right into her, and it took quite some effort for her to pull her eyes away.

"Mr Graeme has just popped out for a moment. Would you mind taking a seat? He shouldn't be long."

Sam sat on the two-seater couch along one wall and picked up a magazine. A couple of times he looked up in the woman's direction. Once he caught her looking back, but after the briefest of pauses, she looked back to her computer screen.

Moments later, a stocky man wearing an expensive looking suit and carrying a briefcase came through the door, marched straight through reception, and into an office on the far side of the room.

After giving her employer a moment to get settled, the woman hit the intercom button. "There's a Sam McKee here to see you Mr Graeme."

"Send him through Lydia. Oh, and make us a pot of coffee would you."

"He's ready for you now Mr McKee."

Sam beamed at her again. "Mr McKee was my father. Please, call me Sam."

Lydia like Sam's direct manner and politeness, something she rarely got from Mr G. "Go on in Sam."

She daydreamed as she watched Sam make his way to Mr G's office. She imagined how nice it would be to have a man with a pleasant manner and knockout smile as a boyfriend, rather than an ill-tempered man like Mr G.

She had hooked up with Mr G hoping to get away from the drudgery of her frugal life. Clichéd she knew, dating the boss, but after losing most of her savings when the finance company she'd invested her savings in crashed during the financial meltdown, she was willing to try almost anything to get back on her feet.

When her last relationship ended, she managed to scrape enough money together to buy out her ex, but soon found the payments too tough and ended up living in a grotty bedsit after having to rent the place out to keep up with the mortgage payments.

She knew a couple of women who'd hooked up with wealthy men, and they seemed happy. She had tried going it alone for a couple of years but look where that had got her.

Shortly after she'd started to work at Graeme Developments, Mr G had begun flirting with her. Lydia, unsure of how to respond, had ignored his advances at first. He wasn't really her type. He was a far harder man than she'd ever dated before, and had an underlying roughness, despite his designer suits. With a strong, solid physique and the nose and scars of a boxer, he wasn't tall and sexy like Sam.

Mr G had been quite charming in the beginning, giving her flowers, and buying her little gifts despite her refusing to go out with him a number of times.

Finally, Lydia relented. It just seemed easier somehow. She'd never dated a wealthy man before and was curious what it would be like. Impressed by the lavish attention, she grew to ignore Mr G's less attractive qualities, hoping his looks would grow on her with time.

When he suggested she join him on a business trip to Europe, she figured what the hell. If things didn't work out, she could always get another job when they got back.

A week after their return from Europe, and before Lydia had had much time to consider the proposition, Mr G insisted she move into his downtown apartment.

Unfortunately, living with Mr G hadn't worked out quite like she'd hoped.

When she first applied to work at Graeme Developments, the recruiter told her she'd be working for a property development company, checking invoices, accounts receivable, contract management, and other related duties. The courses she'd done towards a business diploma, combined with her previous work experience, made her feel fully qualified for the job as described to her by the recruitment agency.

Although a good part of her duties did involve the property development side of Mr G's business, it wasn't until she'd actually started to work for him, that she discovered he also owned a string of brothels. She tried to pretend the brothels were just business, but after moving into Mr G's apartment, this seedy side of Mr G's life started affecting his attitude towards her.

It didn't take long before Mr G reverted to type and was treating her like one of his girls. Sex quickly became part of her job description rather than an act of intimacy and affection between consenting adults. He treated her as if she was only there to fulfil his needs without regard to her own. Lydia felt degraded, undervalued, and worst of all, unloved.

He would come home late at night reeking of booze and cigars, expecting her to wake up and perform like a hooker from one of his clubs. Once he had a few drinks in him, Mr G was a hard man to say no to. Before a month had gone by, she realised her mistake. Not that he ever hit her. He didn't need to. The way he looked at her sometimes was frightening, with a malicious undercurrent itching to escape. She would have to watch her step until she could work out a safe exit strategy. Had her parents still been alive, she might have bolted and stayed with them until she could find another job. But with the bank already pressuring her to catch up with her mortgage arrears, missing even one week's payment would create problems.

If she'd had some financial resources it would have been easy to leave, but despite being given a few pieces of jewellery, a flash watch, and Mr G taking her shopping for clothes on occasion, she had little money to spare. She just needed to hang on until property values went up again. Then she'd be okay. If she sold now, she'd end up with nothing but a bill from the bank.

Sure Mr G paid for most things when they went out on the town, but he also expected her to dress up when they did so. He might pay for $200 bottles of wine and fancy meals at expensive restaurants, but what was left of her income after topping up her mortgage, went on her wardrobe and makeup. If she didn't dress to his expectation, he'd growl at her for being too dowdy. She soon realised that the high-life wasn't all it appeared to be.

Mr G never gave her money unless he knew exactly what she would buy with it, and what he could expect in return. Gilded it may be, but a cage it was nonetheless. If only she'd known. She'd be far happier curled up on the couch with a good thriller and a man who was affectionate and caring, even if he was poor.

Lydia got up from her desk, went into the small kitchen off reception, and turned on the kettle. Eager to see Sam again, she willed it to boil. Once it was bubbling, she filled the plunger and sat it, along with two cups, milk, and sugar, on a chrome and glass tray, and then carried it to Mr G's office.

"Coffee Mr McKee?" Lydia asked, afraid to use Sam's first name in front of her boss.

"Yes thanks, black if you don't mind."

"Boss?"

"No thanks sweetheart. Just leave the tray and close the door on your way out."

Sam admired Lydia's figure as she departed. From Mr G's familiarity with his PA, he reckoned Mr G must be sleeping with her. Not that Sam blamed him. Still, if that were the case, he knew he'd better watch himself. The last thing he needed was a jealous boyfriend on his hands, especially one with a tendency towards violence. Pity, he liked the look of her. Under different circumstance, he might have asked her out.

Sam turned back to Mr G. "So, do you often have items that need recovering?"

"It's rare that someone is stupid enough to steal from me Mr McKee," Mr G said, noting the direction of Sam's gaze.

Sam picked up on Mr G's veiled threat, but chose to ignore it. "Still, you've got the car back now. Not a scratch on her."

"Indeed I do."

Mr G opened a desk drawer and pulled out a two bundles of one-hundred-dollar notes. He smacked them against his palm a couple of times, then threw them on the desk in Sam's direction.

Sam slipped the bundles into the inside pocket of his windbreaker, and got up to go.

Mr G suddenly had a thought. "I don't suppose you play poker by any chance? One of our regulars can't make it this coming Saturday night."

Chapter 4 - Saturday Evening

As Brutus ate his evening meal, the man unloaded the rest of his gear from the white flat-deck truck parked outside. The drive from Christchurch to the small cottage he'd rented on the West Coast, had taken him five and a half hours, including the quick stop he'd made for a late lunch north of Hokitika once he'd hit the coast. The pie had filled him up at the time, but now, like his German shepherd, he was hungry again.

After dumping his suitcase in the larger of the two bedrooms at the back of the house and stacking his other equipment in the hallway, the man went back into the kitchen where Brutus was licking the inside of his empty bowl and put the jug on. The last boxes to unpack were food. Once he'd unloaded and stacked the tins in tidy rows in the pantry, he made himself a cup of tea and sat down at the kitchen table.

The room had seen better days. The bench tops had cuts and scratches etched into their surfaces. The pockmarked lino's bold geometric pattern was out of fashion. Spider webs and grime were thick on the outside of the windows, but for the price, he couldn't complain. Besides, he only planned to be in the area for a few weeks. If he found what he was looking for, he'd be here even less than that.

His hunting plans were different from those of most of the men that rented this place. He wasn't here to shoot pigs or deer like many who made the journey over the Southern Alps to this isolated area. Nor was he interested in looking for pretty stones on the beach, photography, hiking, tramping, or netting whitebait. No, he wanted nothing to do with any of the tourist activities normally associated with the West Coast. He was a hunter, but not of animals, fish, or minerals.

Brutus looked up, his large brown eyes pleading for more food. The man ignored the dog, and after a couple of sips, took his cup of tea into the lounge to get the wood burner going. He needed to heat up water for a bath. His shoulders and lower back ached from the long drive over Arthurs Pass. A good soak would help relieve some of the tension before he started his search in the morning.

Kneeling on the floor, he arranged kindling and newspaper from the wicker basket beside the hearth, into a tidy stack in the burner's firebox. He lit a corner of the paper with a purple Bic from his pocket, and watched as the flames took hold.

While he waited for the water to heat, the man went back into the kitchen, opened a tin of stew, and peeled a couple of potatoes from the bag he'd brought from the supermarket in Greymouth.

Brutus soon gave up waiting for more food, and being tired from spending most of the day standing on the back of the truck, went to lie down by the fire.

As the man stirred his stew, he thought about the photograph of the young girl in his pocket. He couldn't help thinking about it. For years he had carted it around wherever he went, looking at it daily. Now here he was, only two kilometres from where the photo had been taken.

*****

Sam stretched his back. Lifting his elbows high and placing his hands behind his neck, he twisted his torso left then right before lowering his arms and rotating his head around in a circle. It wasn't surprising he was so stiff. He'd been sitting at the poker table for four hours straight.

Opposite the card table, pushed up against the wall, a long narrow sideboard filled with refreshments sat flanked by two over-stuffed chairs. Through an open door down a short hallway to his right, lying on a king-sized bed and propped up with a number of brightly coloured pillows, Sam could see Lydia, dressed in jeans and a loose cotton shirt, reading her book and paying no attention to the seven men playing Texas Holdem metres away in the next room.

Lifting one edge of his hole cards, Sam took a quick peek before counting four $50 chips off the stack in front of him. "Two hundred," he said.

Providing someone hadn't already raised the pot, he always bet four times the big blind whenever he got his favourite hand of Q 10 suited. Today would be no exception.

Seventy percent of the time this tactic paid off, with either the other players folding their hands pre-flop, or by the right cards turning up to make his hand a winner. This move had been a favourite of his father, and had become a family tradition of sorts.

Many poker players are superstitious by nature, and Sam was no different. He always wore sunglasses at the table. He always kept the silver dollar his dad had given him as a souvenir from Las Vegas before he died in his right-hand pocket, and like now, he always bet four times the big blind whenever he was dealt Q 10 suited.

If someone were to ask Sam how much money he'd won with his favourite hand over the years, he wouldn't be able to say. However, he could tell them that of the 230 times he'd been dealt Q 10 suited and bet four times the big blind, he'd taken down the pot 161 times, or 70% of the time, and those were just the sort of odds Sam liked.

After Sam's bet, the man to his left folded, as did the next two players in turn.

Mr G, behind the dealer button, hesitated. He looked at Sam in an attempt to get a read, catching his own reflection in Sam's sunglasses instead. "That's a big bet for someone out of position there Sam. You finally get yourself a hand or are you just making a move?"

Sam looked at his host sitting opposite and smiled. "I rarely bluff Mr G. You should fold now and save yourself some heartache."

Despite his opponent's show of confidence, Mr G had no intention of folding pocket kings. Unless Sam had pocket aces, he would be the firm favourite going into the hand.

Had it been anyone other than Sam, he would have re-raised, but he'd seen the newcomer take down a couple of big pots already that night. Instead, he decided to be cautious and flat call Sam's raise and wait to see if any aces showed up on the board before shoving too much into the middle.

Mr G's hand was steady as he reached for his chips. "Call."

After folds by the small and big blinds, there were only the two of them left in the hand. The chips in the middle were pushed to one side, and three cards were dealt face up in the centre of the table, the jack of clubs, the king of spades and the nine of hearts.

These three cards are called the flop. After another betting round there would be a fourth card (the turn), and finally a fifth (the river), making a total of five communal cards that players could use in any combination with their two hole cards to make the best possible hand.

When Mr G saw that the flop contained a king, matching the two he had face down in front of him, it took him quite some effort not to smile. Now, even if Sam did have pocket aces, his three kings, assuming nothing freakish happened with the next two communal cards, should be good enough to win. As he waited for Sam to bet, Mr G, excited by his trip kings, never even considered the possibility that Sam had flopped a straight. After all, who in their right mind bets $200 out of position with Q 10?

"Three hundred," Sam said, allowing a little tremor to show in his hand as he reached for his chips. Sam figured a moderate continuation bet would either win the pot outright if his opponent hadn't improved, or seem weak enough to entice a raise if he had. With the best possible hand on the table at the moment, either scenario worked for Sam.

The tremor didn't go unnoticed by Mr G.

"Raise to 900," Mr G said, a little too eagerly.

When Sam saw the slight twitch in the corner of Mr G's mouth, he knew Mr G had at least top pair, maybe more. Sam hesitated, but only briefly, before pushing what remained of his stack into the centre of the table. "All in."

Sam hoped Mr G had at least two pair. If so, there was an excellent chance he was in for a nice little payday.

Mr G, convinced his three kings was the best hand on the table, no longer had any reason to hide his smile. He triumphantly tossed his two kings face up onto the table. "Well Sam, I hope you have cab fare home because I call."

"Nice hand," Sam said. "I'll just have to hope you don't pair the board."

Mr G's smile disappeared when Sam's straight hit the felt.

Sam felt like saying 'Of course when I do catch a cab home, there's a 70 percent chance it'll be your money I use to pay the fare', but he knew he had nothing to gain from such a comment. Especially to someone like Mr G. Sam's dad had always taught him to be gracious in victory, for safety's sake if nothing else.

A tinge of red crossed Mr G's face as the last two cards were dealt. Neither player improved his hand, but then Sam didn't need to.

"I thought you might have had me there Mr G," Sam said. "I'm running lucky tonight."

Sam noticed Lydia look up from her book as he stacked his winnings in neat piles. He could have sworn she was suppressing a smile. Odd considering he'd just won the biggest pot of the night against her boyfriend.

Mr G tried to pretend he wasn't a bad loser, but Sam could see his clenched jaw and knew he was steaming. After all the bragging he'd done earlier about the big pots he'd won in previous games, this hand had made him look foolish.

Seeing it was his first game with Mr G and his cronies, Sam had made a point not to win too much from his host early on, instead preferring to take chips off the other players wherever possible. He didn't want to spoil a good thing by irritating the host too early in the evening. But sooner or later he was bound to come up against Mr G in a big hand, so Sam figured he may as well make the most of it.

*****

"Move over you lazy cow," Mr G said when he got to bed sometime after 3:00 a.m. in the morning.

Sweeping the book off the bed onto the floor, he tugged at

the duvet in an attempt to roll Lydia off his side of the king-sized bed.

"What?" she said, her eyes barely opening.

"I said move over. You're taking up the whole bed."

She wriggled over a bit and was snoring lightly again before Mr G's head hit the pillow.

Once settled under the duvet, Mr G considered waking her up, but he was exhausted. Instead, he closed his eyes and tried to slow his racing mind so he could sleep. As he drifted off, different poker hands from the night's game kept replaying over and over in his head, especially the one where Sam had taken him for a packet. He cursed himself for not seeing the possibility Sam had a straight. Then, he cursed his luck that he hadn't paired the board to beat Sam's straight with a full house.

It wasn't like Sam was an ungracious winner or anything. Sam claimed he'd been lucky, and that the cards had just fallen his way, but Mr G wasn't convinced. Sam issued similar platitudes every time he won a decent sized pot.

Mr G knew luck was part of poker, but he also knew that any player relying solely on luck would be cleaned out in short order. To succeed at the game, players needed to stick to strict guidelines, play strong hands in position, and be prepared to throw hands away when they thought they were beaten. Otherwise they'd end up in the crapper before they knew it. Sam playing Q 10 out of position and doubling up through him just ripped his undies. Sam was either a lucky fool, or a lot cleverer than he let on.

Although his brothels made him plenty of money, as did a range of other nefarious activities, Mr G didn't like it when someone, especially one he considered an employee, took his hard-earned cash off him at cards. The plan had been to win back as much of the 20k he'd paid Sam for finding the Mercedes as possible, not have Sam treble his stake over the course of the evening. Mr G considered himself one of life's winners, and Sam McKee had just tainted that image in front of his associates.

As he lay there, he considered ways he might teach Sam a

lesson, a lesson that would show him why others called him Mr G and not just Trevor Graeme. Why he had drivers, secretaries, owned his own penthouse and had two new Mercedes Benz. Why he had men that followed his instructions. Why he was a successful businessman and not some part-time investigator who did odd jobs. Why he was on top of the pile, and Sam was lurking somewhere nearer the bottom. And most importantly, why he was a winner and Sam was just too damn lucky for his own good.

Chapter 5 - Wednesday Morning

It was just getting light when Sam pulled into the empty parking area at the beach end of Burke Road. Being the first person to arrive at the popular jade-hunting location was important, and meant that he would have first crack at finding whatever the king tides had exposed overnight.

After locking his car, he waded across a small S-shaped creek and made his way down to the beach. Once at the high tide mark, he turned right and walked parallel to the water, facing into the light northerly breeze. His eyes scanned left, then right, then back again, as he searched for glimmers of green amongst the disturbed material along the edge of the shingle bank. A glossy green could indicate the existence of the calcium rich nephrite jade, or greenstone as it's called by many of the locals, that washes up on the beaches of New Zealand's West Coast.

If a pebble caught his eye, he would excavate around it with the toe of his gumboot, further exposing the item. If it still looked promising, he'd reach down and pick it up, turning it over in his hand for closer inspection, and rubbing it against his trousers to dry off any residual moisture. Most of the pebbles he picked up dried grey rather than staying green. These he dropped again as soon as it became obvious that they were mainly quartz or some other common mineral and not the jade he sought.

The beach was relatively flat below the high tide mark, but the shingle bank was narrow and rose steeply towards the flaxes, native grasses, and other plants that grew along the top. These plants fought hard for a foothold in the harsh salt-laden ground. In some areas, the tide had carried away much of the shingle, exposing a reddish soil layered with shells and rock.

Sam knew that middens — piles of shells and other waste products from old foraging expeditions by Māori or early Europeans — containing artefacts were sometimes found in this area so, if he noticed a thicker than normal layer of shells, he would walk further up beach to investigate.

Although Sam had found the odd artefact during his frequent jade hunting expeditions, he'd never found a real prize. He'd seen *mere* and *patu* (war clubs) as well as adzes and other primitive tools that had been found by others in similar locations. Most were now in museums, but he'd never had the joy of unearthing one himself.

One private collection he'd seen here on the West Coast had contained not only buckets of jade stones and pebbles, but also a number of adzes and other stone tools the collector had found after walking hundreds of miles, over many years, on this very same beach.

As Sam walked, the wave action to his left churned the beach gravel, creating a clattering sound like a thousand castanets. This tumbling process also helped polish the jade pebbles he was looking for.

Originally, the jade, or *pounamu* as Māori indigenous to New Zealand call it, found in the local rivers has a whitish rind on it, and looks nothing like the richly coloured green stone people see carved into *koru*, *tiki*, and other jewellery.

During times of flood, some of this jade washes down the rivers into the sea, where it's tossed and tumbled for thousands of years. Gradually, the rind that hides the stone's inner beauty gets worn away, revealing its translucent green interior.

Over the eons, the combined action of the tides, currents, and waves transport pieces of jade hundreds of kilometres from the rivers of their origin. After decades of polishing by the abrasive gravel and sand, and rumbling around in countless storms, some of the stones wash up onto the beach, to be exposed at some future date for jade hunters like Sam to find.

This process has turned some West Coast beaches into a natural jewellery box, with semi-precious gemstones lying there for the taking ... if only one knows where, when, and what to look for.

Along the high tide mark is the most likely place to spot such treasure. Jade, having a higher specific gravity than most of the other rocks on the beach, is sometimes left behind after the lighter materials are dragged back into the sea when the tide retreats.

Sam concentrated as he walked. After half an hour or so, he spotted a small glimmer of green nestled next to a couple of rounded pieces of white quartz, and bent over to retrieve it. The 50mm long pebble was about half as wide, but only 5mm thick, its edges worn smooth by the sea. When he held it towards the sky between his thumb and forefinger, he could see the light shining through it. Although small, it was a lovely piece of jade. Having a slightly lighter than normal colour, Sam suspected the pebble had travelled up the coast from the Arahura River, over seventy kilometres away.

He rubbed the jade against the side of his nose to give it a light coating of the ultra-fine oil found on that section of a human's skin; a trick once used by watchmakers to lubricate timepieces before advent of modern lubricants. A smile crossed his face when he saw how it glistened. After a final inspection, he slipped his find into the top pocket of his Swandri and buttoned it safely away. Once the piece had a small hole drilled through it, and a woven cord attached, it would make a lovely necklace for someone.

A hundred metres further on, he came to another stream. It wasn't that deep but the speed of the water had cut a deep channel into the softer sand, exposing the many coloured pebbles that lined its bottom. He knew this was a good place to find jade. Anywhere less dense materials could wash away, uncovering the heavier jade left behind was a good spot to find the treasure he sought. When the sunlight is at the right angle, a piece of jade can shine like a beacon when submerged under a few inches of water, making it easy to distinguish from the duller pebbles around it.

The water rushed halfway up his gumboots when Sam stepped into the stream. He could feel its tug as he searched up and down the ten-metre wide channel. A few interesting looking pebbles caught his attention. A lovely piece of smoky grey quartz, another rose-coloured, and two almost clear pebbles, were quickly snapped up. These pieces he'd use around his potted cacti for decoration, or polish in his mechanical tumbler.

He slipped off his day-pack and dropped the stones into a side pouch along with some others he pulled from his trouser pocket. Sam couldn't remember the last time he went for a walk along a beach and didn't fill his pockets. There was always something interesting to pick up, even when there wasn't any jade around.

It took him ten minutes to inspect the stream. Once satisfied there was nothing to be found, he left it behind and moved further along the beach. After picking up another piece of quartz, he turned to look back down the beach. Far in the distance a man and large dog were heading in his direction. Another jade-hunter most likely, the West Coast was full of them. Glad he'd gotten up early, he moved off, resuming his slow amble, his head swaying back and forth, then back again, as it swept along the line of the tide.

When the beach turned sandy, he picked up his pace. There'd be no jade here, but once he rounded the point a few hundred meters on, he knew the beach would turn back to shingle and the hunt would begin again.

As he walked, he remembered the hand of poker that had enabled this little excursion and smiled. Mr G was a reasonable player, but Sam felt the man's ego got in the way of sound decision making at times. He hadn't learned to stop and think 'what can beat me'? A player's biggest losses often come when they have a good hand, so that's the time players need to calculate carefully, and give their opponents some respect. In poker, mistakes are costly. There is no prize for second place.

Mr G's lack of respect for Sam had cost him dearly. He underestimated the ability of the other players, and he wasn't skilled enough at working out the odds. This meant Mr G often over or under bet his hand. Luckily for Sam, his cronies were even worse. Still Sam wasn't complaining. Once he'd paid all his bills, and knocked a few grand off his mortgage, he'd won enough to get him and his vehicle across Cook Strait plus enough to pay for food, accommodation, and expenses for the rest of the summer should he desire.

How long he stayed in the area would depend on how the hunting went. If he found good quantities of jade he'd hang around. If not, he might try his luck panning for gold in Otago, or maybe head further south and hunt for garnets at a spot a friend had mentioned.

But so far, things were looking pretty good. Finding a piece of jade before lunch on the first day had to be a good omen. And there was so much more beach to explore.

Once he got around the point, Sam lost sight of the other jade-hunter, not that he cared. He enjoyed the solitude. Some days he wouldn't see another soul all day, especially the wet ones.

It was often wet on the Coast, but Sam didn't mind the rain. West Coasters often said that if it wasn't for the rain and the sand flies every bastard would want to live here. Sam tended to agree with them. His love of the coast made him feel like a local at times. He certainly came down whenever he got the chance. Where else could you go for a walk along the beach and come home with jewellery quality stones that needed nothing done to them apart from having a small hole drilled in them? Besides, as he'd discovered on more than one occasion, jade was easier to spot when wet.

Today however, the rain had stayed away ... well so far anyway. After walking for another 30 minutes or so, he came to a second creek, slightly smaller than the previous one. Beyond the creek, a couple of hundred meters inland, on a slight rise off to his right, a twisted Rata stood, branches like arms outstretched against a cloud specked sky as if getting ready to brace itself against its next battering from the wind and rain.

He caught the sound of cows lowing as they grazed on the lush paddocks between the beach and the main road. When he lifted his head and inhaled deeply, he could smell their rich scent.

After checking out the stones along the one side of the creek, Sam pulled a muesli bar out of his daypack took a big bite. Fossicking made him hungry. The muesli bar wouldn't satisfy his hunger for long.

After searching the far side of the creek without luck, he turned south and headed back towards his car. He closed his eyes briefly and imagined the smell of hot coffee and bacon. His stomach demanded more food, gurgling and growling at him while he walked.

The tide had turned and was moving higher and higher up the beach. Every few minutes a wave, slightly bigger than the last, would race towards him, forcing him to sprint for higher ground or risk a drenching. He'd have a lunch-break, and come back out later in the afternoon once high tide had passed.

Walking in a southward direction the view was quite different. The Alps followed an arc around the coast to the southwest, snow still covering their tops despite the weather getting warmer. It always amazed him how close to the sea the mountains were. The air was so clear he could make out ridges and rock formations on peaks over a hundred kilometres away.

As he gazed down the long expanse of beach, he half expected to see the man with the dog again, but there was no sign of him. The wind had started to get up. Maybe the man had tired of walking into it.

Sam on the other hand, with the wind now at his back, was pleased he'd chosen to walk north early on while the wind was light. Now, as it strengthened, it would help push him back towards his car and save him energy.

He remembered what he'd read about the early Pacific explorers as he walked, still scanning left and right. The early navigators always sailed as close to the wind as possible. Then, when they got tired, thirsty, or were running out of supplies, they could turn around and run downwind, all the way home. As the gusts blew him towards his car, he saw the sense in their methods.

He made good time down the beach. Occasionally, a gust would lift the dry sand off the beach and pepper him with it. However, that didn't worry Sam. Having done his stint into the wind, he just lifted the hood of his parka, and with his broad back acting as both sail and protection, made his way homeward with little discomfort.

When Sam hit the sandy patch of beach again he picked up his pace. Halfway down the stretch where a small indentation jutted into the coastline, possibly the mouth of an ancient creek, he noticed a section of the metre high bank had collapsed spilling a large quantity of shells onto the shingle at its base. He hadn't noticed the collapse on his way past the first time.

He shook his head and scrunched his eyebrows.

I must have been looking towards the point when I went by. Hard to believe I missed this.

Even from twenty metres away, he could tell this was a spot worth investigation. What looked to be a large concentration of a *pipi* shells gave all the indications of an old midden. And middens, as any good fossicker knew, can contain all sorts of interesting items that have been left behind, or inadvertently dropped by those who'd camped and feasted here hundreds of years previously.

As he walked towards the pile of shells to investigate further in the hopes of finding an artefact of some sort, he noticed a set of boot prints heading in the same direction. The prints looked fresh. Whoever had made them had done so earlier that day.

"Bugger, someone's beaten me to it," he mumbled. But as he neared the pile of shells, he saw the stranger's tracks head up the bank just before the point where it had collapsed.

That's odd.

Sam followed the prints up and along the edge of the bank until they were just above the spot where the shells spilled onto the rocks below. One footprint disappeared and to the right, a handprint took its place.

Whoever it was has climbed up here and walked along the edge. Their weight must have caused the bank to slip.

Bending down he inspected the indentations, fingering the soft soil.

This looks like where his knee landed when the bank collapsed ... and there's a handprint where he pushed himself back to his feet. He must not have noticed the pile of shells he inadvertently exposed.

Sam stood and looked inland over the low scrub and

paddocks towards the main road about a kilometre away. The white flash of a campervan appeared briefly on the road in the distance, followed by the silver rush of a milk tanker.

The footprints carried on into the scrubland and disappeared towards a patch of gorse. It wasn't until Sam turned to head back towards the pile of shells that he noticed some very large paw prints in a patch of sandy soil just beyond the collapse. He hadn't noticed any dog prints down on the beach.

The dog must have been running around up on the shingle, and joined the man once he'd climbed up the bank. Maybe the man got caught short. That pocket of scrub over there would be a good spot if you needed some privacy.

Whatever the case, the pair had obviously gone back to the beach by a different route because Sam couldn't see any return prints. It would also explain why the midden was still untouched.

On his way back to the midden, Sam picked up a stout branch. With it, he started digging into the pile of shells. It was quite a pile. Whoever had camped here all those years ago had had quite a feast, possibly over a period of weeks or even months. Some of the shells showed signs of fire, and as he got further into the pile, more charcoal began to emerge.

Sam could feel his heart rate elevate and his breathing become more rapid, both from the excitement of his discovery, and from exertion as he dug further into the biggest midden he'd ever come across.

When one end of a slightly larger object emerged from the compacted shell and ash pit, Sam caught his breath. What he saw looked like a handle of some sort, but it wasn't greenstone. Although the item had all the characteristics of bone, it seemed a little too dark. He put down his stick and carefully dug away at the material around the object with his fingers. Once he'd exposed enough of the item to get a firm grip on it, he gently wriggled it back and forth while pulling it from the surrounding mass of shells.

Then, as he leaned back using his bodyweight as additional

leverage, the object came out with a rush dumping him on his backside.

He looked down at the object in his hand and was delighted to see a foot-long broad-bladed fighting club or patu as Māori call them. A scrap of the woven flax cord, used to secure the club to a warrior's wrist during battle, poked through a hole near the top of the club's handle, and wrapped around the handle a number of times where it narrowed before widening again to form the blade.

"Well I'll be buggered," he said as he brushed the loose sand and broken pieces of shell off the heavy war-club.

Clutching it by the handle, Sam tapped the patu's edge softly against the palm of his hand. The weight was significant. He could imagine how lethal it would become when swung with any force.

Unlike other patu he'd seen, this one had no decoration on its blade. Around the narrowest part of its handle, partially covered with the decaying flax cord, were a series of grooves designed to keep the cord from slipping up or down the handle.

The grain of the hardwood used to make the club was very fine, and he could understand why he thought it was bone at first glance. Much of the wood's original colour had bleached out over time, giving it an appearance similar to those he'd seen made from whalebone.

Sam closed his eyes and had a brief fantasy he'd find more artefacts, or the Holy Grail itself, a jade mere. He knew the likelihood of that was slim, but treasure hunters are like people who buy lottery tickets, and dreaming is all part of the fun.

Historically, most fighting clubs were made of wood, bone, or some other less precious stone like shale or serpentine. Only the most prestigious and fearsome warriors carried mere made of pounamu. None the less, a wooden patu was deadly in the hands of an experienced man.

Sam couldn't believe his luck in finding one. He hefted the club once again, and imagined swinging it in battle. When all the weight of a war-club came down on its narrow edge, the force would have cracked open a man's skull as easily as breaking an egg on the edge of a frying pan.

How had this fine weapon come to be left behind? Was it just an oversight, or was the owner surprised by a rival raiding party?

Sam climbed to higher ground to have another look around for the man and his dog. The land was reasonably flat, and apart from the odd patch of scrub, he had a reasonable view all the way to the road. When he saw no one, he figured the pair must have circled back to the car park by some other route.

He smiled, happy to have the place to himself, then ducked back down to the midden and got to work. He saw no point in standing around like a meerkat on lookout advertising his location and the fact that he was on to something.

From the sheer size of this midden, he knew he'd need a bit of time to investigate it fully. It would also be worth probing around its edges for anything else that may have been left behind. If those who created this midden had to leave in a hurry because they were under attack, they could have dropped all sorts of tools in their haste to get moving. Often occupants around such a camp would have scrapers, adzes, stone drills, bone needles and other common implements.

After digging around a little more and finding nothing, Sam turned to check how the tide was doing. He could see that the waves were really starting to race a fair distance up the beach now and realised it was time for him to head back to his car.

But before he went, he wanted to protect the location of his discovery from others. He needed to work quickly if he was going to get back to his car before the tide got too high for him to walk safely along the narrow beach, between the shingle bank and the thundering sea.

The incoming tide would wash most of his footprints away as soon as it reached its highpoint. Any prints leading to the midden that were above the high tide mark would need to be disguised somehow to stop them from attracting unwanted attention should someone wander by before he had a chance to return.

When another deep rumbling erupted from his stomach, he knew he'd be ravenous by the time he tidied up here and made the hour-long journey back to his car.

Sam slipped the patu into his backpack. Then he walked onto the flats and broke a branch off a scrubby tree to use as a broom, planning to sweep away the footsteps leading up to the midden from the beach.

After returning to the excavation site, he flattened the pile of shells he'd uncovered and methodically covered them with a layer of stones. After sprinkling handfuls of dry sand over the fresh earth, blending it into its surroundings, he walked backwards while holding the branch and swept back and forth obscuring the footprints, until his gumboots were in the wash of the incoming surf. Looking back at his handwork, he smiled at what he saw, and tossed his makeshift broom into the sea. Once the tide was full in little more than an hour, there'd be little sign he was ever here.

Standing at the edge of the surf, Sam looked around for three reference points he could use to triangulate the spot, enabling him to find it again. A large driftwood log 150 metres to the south, driven well above the current high tide mark by a storm would be one. The stand of scrub, towards where the man and the dog's footprints had headed, would be another, and the ancient Matai tree, 100 meters inland, would be the third.

He looked at all three landmarks and tried to emblazon his current location relative to them in his memory. He'd be devastated if he couldn't find the spot again, and with mile after mile of similar looking terrain, not finding the spot again was a real possibility if he wasn't careful.

After satisfying himself that his reference points were firmly set in his mind, he readjusted his backpack and headed south towards his car, his eyes sweeping left and right in the manner of the forever-hopeful jade hunter.

Half an hour down the beach, he thought he saw people walking in his direction, but as he got closer, the figures he'd seen turned out to be the twisted branches of yet another large tree washed down some flooded river and later driven ashore.

Before long, Sam came to the small creek that ran across the beach below where he'd parked his car. After wading across, he unlocked his vehicle and climbed in, out of the ever-strengthening wind.

With his daypack on the floor of the passenger side, he checked himself in the rear-view mirror. A reddish face returned his gaze. Making a note to put some sun-block on when he got back to his rented cottage, he put the Toyota in gear and drove off towards the batch with his booty.

*****

Mr G squeezed the phone like he was trying to strangle a chicken. "Look, I don't give a shit. If you can't control the girls and keep the books straight, I'll find someone who can." He slammed down the receiver and turned towards the door. "Lydia, get your arse in here."

Lydia sighed as she rose from her chair. As she picked up her notebook, she cursed Mr G under her breath, wishing she had the nerve to say something to his face.

She hated it when Mr G was like this. He'd been grumpy ever since Saturday night's poker game.

Normally when things went wrong, Mr G's grumpiness wore off in a day or two, but here it was halfway through the week and he was still acting like a petulant child.

She had to admit he'd lost a lot of money, but that was no excuse to take it out on her. She couldn't help grinning when she remembered the exclamations from the other players when Sam turned over his cards. The inevitable post-hand analysis had followed. Not that the others were critical of Mr G's play. No, they were all bright enough to know that that wouldn't be a clever move. Their comments were mainly conciliatory. 'Bad luck Mr G' and 'Shit Mr G, how could you know Sam had a straight' and comments like that. Had the loser been one of the others, they might have said 'ha ha, you just got your arse whipped', but not when it was Mr G. Their arse-licking made

Lydia sick.

She'd seen the way Mr G's cronies behaved around him on numerous occasions. None of them had the guts to tell him the truth, tell him he needed to learn a little respect for the other players at the table. He needed to learn that he wasn't invincible, or quite the winner he considered himself to be.

Still, she couldn't talk. Many times she'd wanted to speak up but hadn't had the nerve.

His bullying tactics didn't gain him respect or loyalty. It just made people do what Mr G wanted to save themselves from an ear bashing, a beating, or worse, while cursing him in private.

She'd caught Sam's eye briefly when he raked in the huge pile of chips. Lydia wondered if he'd noticed her little smile. He obviously had a few clues when it came to diplomacy. Mr G would have reacted badly if Sam had rubbed salt in his financial wounds, but Sam's reaction to the big win had been surprisingly respectful, as if he'd somehow known about Mr G's nasty streak.

Had the game occurred on any other night, she would have missed the show. The weekly games were usually played in a hotel room somewhere, or in the back room of Mr G's club. But that night, Mr G had opted to play host in his Wellington penthouse.

She'd been excited when she heard Mr G invite Sam to the game. So, rather than going to a movie as she often did on a Saturday night while Mr G played cards, she decided to stay home and eavesdrop.

She retired to the bedroom when the players arrived, leaving her bedroom door half-open so she could hear what transpired in the other room. With luck, she'd also get the odd peek at Sam.

Usually, when engrossed in a book, it would take an earthquake or something of similar magnitude to drag her away from it, but having Sam in the next room distracted her. She found herself reading a page or two before stopping to listen, hoping to catch Sam's voice. Occasionally, she'd look up and catch a glimpse of him on the far side of the table, partially hidden by Mr G's back.

Why did this man make her feel like a teenager again? It had to be more than just his rugged good looks. For some reason she felt relaxed in his presence, safe even, a contrast to the tension she always felt in Mr G's company these days. Whatever it was, she liked the way her stomach fluttered when Sam was nearby.

When the big hand went down, it was hard for Lydia to miss hearing their comments.

"Phewwww," one had gasped. "I didn't expect that!"

Others had commented too. She'd looked up from her book and seen Sam shake his head as if shocked that he'd won the hand.

"Wow, thought you might have had me there Mr G."

She was pleased Sam had the sense to show some diplomacy. Lydia had waited to see what Mr G's reaction would be to the big loss, whether he'd get angry or not. Although Sam was taller than most of the men at the table, his broad shoulders sitting inches above the paunchy and softer looking men on either side of him, Lydia knew Mr G was tough enough to give Sam some trouble were there to be a physical confrontation. Uncharacteristically, Mr G had said little after the loss.

Lydia remembered watching Sam's face as he stacked his chips. His skin was clear and bronzed from time spent outdoors. A day's stubble graced his strong jaw line. When she noticed his mouth twitch at the corners, she could have sworn he was suppressing a smile.

"Lydia. I said get your arse in here!"

Lydia shook herself out of her daydream and started towards Mr G's door. "Sorry boss, what can I do for you?"

"I need you to book me a flight to Auckland. One of my managers is an incompetent plonkwad and if I don't go and sort things out, I'm going to go broke."

"When did you want to fly out?"

"This afternoon. Oh and book my normal suite. Tell them I might need to stay a couple of nights. I'll text you when I want you to book the return flight. Once you've done that, nip home and pack me a bag. I have a lunch meeting."

Lydia tried not to smile until she'd left Mr G's office. The idea of a couple days peace and quiet without a demanding boss and ungracious lover around would be as good as a holiday. With luck, she might have time to finish reading her book. With even more luck, Mr G's plane might crash.

Chapter 6 - Wednesday Afternoon

Sam pulled into a narrow entranceway obscured from the highway by a row of large flax bushes. After driving down a steep driveway that cut through a patch of native bush, he came to a small clearing and a one-roomed batch built hard up against a rocky outcrop. A plastic rainwater tank stood next to the batch on a stumpy platform of lichen covered wood. A dilapidated outbuilding, further back on the section, contained a long-drop and woodshed.

He parked the Toyota Hi-Lux beside the water tank, and got out. Carrying his daypack, he scrunched along a path of crushed shells that led to a weather-beaten door. Old fishing floats, and strings of shells and driftwood, were mounted on the batch's bright blue walls completing the seaside decor.

To the left of the building, the ground dropped away to mussel covered rocks, and an angry sea. Gusts of wind caused the wave tops to become streaks of white spray as they crashed into the shoreline, and seabirds struggled to land on a pair of small rocky islands 100 metres from shore.

After kicking off his gumboots, Sam unlocked the door and shouldered his way into the room. He dropped his daypack on the wooden table opposite the coal range and filled the kettle from a tap above the sink. Reaching under the bench he turned on the gas bottle, lit the burner that sat down one end of the stainless steel bench, and placed the kettle on it to boil.

As the kettle heated, he rummaged through the cardboard box of supplies he'd bought from the supermarket on his way through the previous day, and found a jar of instant coffee and some powdered milk. He put a little of each into one of the mugs he found hanging on hooks above the sink-bench, and then grabbed a loaf of bread and a block of cheese. By the time he'd finished making two thick sandwiches, the kettle was whistling.

Sitting at the table to eat, he undid the flap of his shirt and rummaged around for the small piece of jade he'd found. He took the other stones he'd collected on his walk from the side pouch of his daypack and lined them up along the window ledge where the sunlight would strike them.

With a sense of reverence, Sam pulled the patu out of his bag, carefully laying it on the table next to the piece of jade so he could admire it while he ate.

Once he'd finished his first sandwich, he reached for the newspaper and flicked through the pages looking for the tide chart. Low tide had been at 6:03 a.m. that morning.

Sam checked his watch. It was just after midday, so the tide would start heading out again soon. That gave him just enough time for a siesta before he returned to the beach.

He stretched out on the bed, hands locked behind his head, and listened to the sound of the sea. As he relaxed, his thoughts returned to the man with the dog. He wondered why, assuming the man had just nipped into the bushes to relieve himself, he hadn't returned to the beach by the same path. Surely, coming back down the old creek bed would have been easier than striking out across ankle-twisting scrubland. Sam also wondered what breed of dog it was. It had looked large from a distance, but when he saw the size of the paw print in the loose soil he'd been surprised how big it was. The dog was a monster, and if the depth of the print was anything to go by, it hadn't missed many meals either.

Despite the questions running though his mind, the sound of the waves soon lulled him to dreamlike state. Before long, he was picturing himself digging into the midden and finding a ceremonial mere of pounamu and other artefacts — he saw stones on a beach of glittering green as he strolled in sunshine that was just that much brighter than in real life.

When the rumbling sound of a milk tanker woke him up two hours later, he was well rested from his early morning adventure, and keen to get back on the treasure trail.

He splashed some cold water onto his face and pulled on some clean socks. A grin crossed his face when he looked out the window and saw that the wind had dropped and shifted a little to the west. The crests of the waves weren't being blown horizontal like they had been earlier. This would make his afternoon much more enjoyable. He noticed some dark cumulous clouds out to sea, so he dug his oilskin out of the suitcase on the floor next to the bed, and stuffed it into his daypack along with a bottle of water, a few muesli bars, and an apple.

Hefting the pack over his shoulder, Sam stepped into his trusty Red Band gumboots. As he wriggled his toes, he wondered how many beach-miles he'd done in them. They were, by far, the best footwear for this type of expedition, with a strong stiff sole that didn't flex too much when walking over the lumpy ground, good deep tread for grip in the sand, and shin-high protection from the many small creeks and the occasional waves his feet would be exposed to. They might look clunky, yet when combined with a thick pair of woollen socks, he found them perfect for the stony conditions he'd encounter on the beach.

As he drove north along the coast, Sam could see the ocean off to his left. Lines of waves marched towards land on their way across the Tasman Sea. He slowed when he saw the sign indicating the Burke Road turnoff, and then veered left onto a single-lane gravel road pointing straight towards the beach.

A pair of brightly coloured pukeko skittered out of his way, half running and half flying across the road, their furiously beating dark-blue wings lifting their orange legs and feet just clear of the four-strand wire fence. Cows in the paddock lifted their heads briefly to check out the birds arrival, but were soon munching grass again.

Near the end of the road, the deck of a flat bed truck protruded from behind a pile of shingle in the parking area. He frowned at the thought of not having the beach to himself. He wanted to explore the midden without there being prying eyes around. If this was a serious jade hunter, and they were heading in the same direction, much of his time before the light faded may be spent waiting for whoever it was to leave before he could get down to the serious business of excavation.

"Bugger." Sam grumbled. He grabbed his daypack off the

back seat and went around to the rear door to get the folding shovel he always kept in the vehicle. Slipping the shovel through the loops on the side of the daypack, he tightened a pair of straps to hold it in place. "I hope you've gone south whoever you are."

After locking the vehicle and wading across the small creek, he walked down to the beach with fingers crossed hoping that whoever owned the truck had turned south for their walk, rather than north towards his discovery. When he arrived at the high tide mark, Sam looked for footprints or any sign of the truck's owner. He saw nothing.

Breathing a sigh of relief, he automatically adopted his left to right, and back again scanning technique, looking for jade as he walked. The tide, although receding, was still relatively high and he had to dodge the occasional wave as he marched north.

As Sam rounded a small point where the beach broadened out and sand replaced the shingle, his face dropped. Two sets of footprints, one the deep tread of a boot, the other those of a very large dog, trailed up the beach in the direction of the midden.

*****

When Mr G exited the Auckland airport terminal, Jimmy was waiting to take him to his hotel. After relieving Mr G of his overnight bag, he led the way outside to where he'd parked the car.

Mr G got in the back seat and settled in for the trip into the central city. "God I hate the traffic here. I can't understand how you people put up with it day after day."

"I've got *The Herald* if you'd like to read the newspaper, Mr G."

"No thanks, Jimmy, just get me to the hotel."

Mr G closed his eyes and tried to relax. He knew it would be a long night. By the time he settled into his room, grabbed a bite to eat, and drove to his premises in Queen Street, it would be close to 8:00 p.m. How long it would take to sort out the shambles he'd find once he got there was anyone's guess.

As Jimmy pulled up to the entrance of the hotel, a doorman rushed up to the car and opened the door. "Welcome sir. Please, step this way."

Jimmy popped the boot and retrieved Mr G's bag.

Mr G slapped a banknote into his hand. "I'll give you a call in a couple of hours Jimmy boy. We've got some tidying up to do later on."

Jimmy nodded. "Sure thing, Mr G. I'm only 10 minutes away when you need me."

With bag in hand, Mr G made his way through the glass and chrome revolving door. The young woman at reception had his key ready by the time he'd crossed the lobby.

"Nice to see you again, Mr Graeme. Let me know if there's anything you need."

"Thanks, I will."

Once in his suite, Mr G dumped his bag in the bedroom and sat down on one of the plush burgundy armchairs by the window. He fished around in his pocket for his phone, and then dialled.

From where he sat, he could see his reflection in the oval mirror on the wall opposite. Deep lines creased his face, and dark bags from a lack of sleep underlined his eyes. "You look stressed Trevor. These incompetent dickheads will be the death of you."

When Ethan answered the phone, Mr G turned away from the mirror and looked out over the cityscape fifteen floors below.

"It's me," Mr G said. "I've just arrived in town."

"Hi Mr G, to what do I owe this pleasure?"

"As if you didn't know you snot gobbling little arse wipe."

"That's hardly fair, Mr G."

"Shut the fuck up and listen. I'm going to have a shower, and grab a bite to eat. Then I'm heading your way. You'd better hope everything is up to scratch. If not, you'll wish you'd caught the first available flight out of the country. Get my drift sunshine?"

*****

Lydia shuffled the papers on her desk into a neat pile, and then took her coffee cup to the sink, giving it a quick rinse before leaving it turned upside down on the bench. After setting the phone system to divert any calls to her cell in case Mr G or one of his clients rang, she locked the door, and headed home.

Looking after Mr G had become her main job since she'd moved into his apartment, a personal assistant with benefits. Not the job she'd imagined doing at this stage of her life. But at least with Mr Misery Guts out of town, she could forget about him for a while. There was no reason for her to stay in the office. Besides, she had a hot date with the thriller she'd been reading.

The main character in the book reminded her of Sam. The only difference being that in *Bad Chillies*, the man with the sparkling blue eyes was a cop, and Sam McKee was certainly not one of those. Still, she had this feeling that regardless of which side of the law Sam found himself on, he was a good man. Maybe it was the way he smiled, or the way his eyes sparkled. In either case, Lydia's instincts told her that only good could reside in those deep clear pools of blue, unlike the malevolent and often bloodshot sockets Mr G used to stare his underlings into submission.

Now that Mr G wasn't watching her every move, she felt lighter, more carefree. She hadn't realised how submissive she'd become. How she'd changed from the self-assured woman she'd once been, into a person she hardly recognised.

As the elevator doors closed, Lydia hit the button for the ground floor lobby. She felt the weight of Mr G's foul temper over the last few days, lift from her shoulders as she descended. The stainless steel walls of the lift reflected her smile. It was time for a nice relaxing evening with no grumpy man-child to worry about.

By the time she exited the building on Manners Street and started the three-block stroll towards Taranaki Street, where the apartment was located, she had a spring in her step that she hadn't felt in ages.

A couple of blocks further down, she stopped at a convenience store and bought a small carton of milk and a chocolate bar before turning left down Taranaki Street towards home.

Mr G's apartment was one of two on the top floor of a building half-way down the block. From the lounge and master bedroom, Lydia could see the inner harbour and Te Papa, the national museum. Further to the north, over the top of a large brick Harbour Board building, recently converted to a micro brewery and bar, she could see the container terminal, and beyond that, the Petone foreshore on the far side of the harbour.

Of all the things she liked about the apartment, the view of the harbour was her favourite. She'd spend hours in the big chair by the window, reading or watching the activity on the water. Multiple ferries, and countless other vessels, came in and out of the harbour each day. Often on weekends there were yacht races. She remembered reading in the local paper that more than 90 cruise ships were scheduled to visit Wellington this summer. Lydia often imagined herself being aboard one of them, sailing far away.

With the milk in the fridge, Lydia grabbed her book from the bedside table and went into the ensuite to fill the spa bath. Placing her book within easy reach on the edge of the vanity, she returned to the bedroom and removed her shoes and hung up her office clothes. Re-entering the now steamy bathroom in her underwear, she flipped on the switch for the extractor fan and bent down to test the water temperature. After making an adjustment, she grabbed a bottle of bubble bath from a shelf above the vanity, and poured a good measure into the rising water.

The marble tiles were cool against her feet as she dropped her bikini briefs and bra onto the floor, and stepped gingerly into the steaming tub. She eased herself down, and settled back, her long hair streaming in the water. A blissful "ahhh" escaped her mouth as she closed her eyes, and the luxuriant warmth surrounded her.

After a 10 minute soak, she reached for her book, eager to find out more about the blue-eyed cop in her novel. Would he and his partner find the missing kids, or would they be brutalised by the sadistic kidnapper?

*****

Sam stopped when he saw the two sets of prints. They were definitely fresh. The high tide mark was further up the beach. These prints were in damp sand recently exposed by the tide.

He tried to focus though the salt-laden spray getting blown across the beach by the moderate westerly. In the distance were vague shapes, possibly those of a man and his dog, but from this far away, it was hard to be sure. The curve of the beach and the misty haze made seeing more than half a kilometre or so ahead difficult.

Shimmering mirages and driftwood logs often looked like people from a distance. The only solution he had was to pick up the pace, follow the tracks, and see if he could close the gap. Then, he might be able to get some idea of what they were doing.

The shoreline was in a constant state of flux, which is exactly what jades hunters want. No two days are the same as the waves shifted the shingle and debris around with every new tide.

If the man was looking for jade, Sam wondered if he'd head back near the midden. But was he a jade hunter or just someone out walking his dog? Surely a typical dog-walker wouldn't be back out on the beach again so soon.

Sam didn't want to get too close until he had a better idea what was going on. He certainly didn't want the man to see him near the midden. Most likely there would be a simple explanation about the man's inland foray earlier that morning. But what if there wasn't? And what if the dog was as mean as he was big?

Sam was confident he could defend himself against the man if need be, but dogs, especially big ones like this, had always given him the shits. People you could reason with, but big dogs … well they were different. You were either a friend and in danger of drowning in slobber, or you were an enemy. A lot of dogs snarl and snap if they decide they don't like the look of you, but big dogs are dangerous and unpredictable. Sam had the evidence on his right arm to prove it.

For a moment, he rubbed his old scar as he walked, but before long his mind wandered back to the chase. He found the pace invigorating and was making much better time than he had earlier in the day when he'd been scanning the ground for jade, not that he wasn't still looking, it was just that any piece he was likely to find while walking at this pace would have to be laying flat and in plain view, unobscured by the other pebbles around it.

Every hundred metres or so, he looked up to gauge how much ground he'd gained on his quarry.

Out to sea, the rainclouds he'd spotted earlier were a little closer, but they didn't look like they'd create a problem any time soon. He figured with the wind having dropped, he'd have a couple of hours before he'd need to ditch his lightweight parka for his oilskin. Still, it was the West Coast. The weather didn't always do what you expected. Usually it was either raining, or about to rain. If a person didn't have good waterproof gear they didn't last long this side of the Southern Alps.

Sam didn't slow his pace to check the first creek he came to for jade. He was too intent on catching up with the pair ahead.

Once past the creek, he crested a slight rise where the shingle had been pushed into a heap during a recent storm. From this vantage point he could see two figures less than 500 metres ahead. The man was carrying a pack of some sort, marching stoically onward. Meanwhile, the dog roamed free, running up the shingle bank to the edge of scrub, and then back down again, plunging into the froth as the waves raced up the beach. The dog was fast and powerful, and created quite a wake as it ploughed into the surf. From this distance, it looked like a German shepherd. If so, it was the largest one he'd ever seen.

Sam's accelerated pace slowed. Now his focus was on the pair ahead, and what they were doing rather than catching up with them. Sure, he could be passing greenstone at every step, but rarely did his eyes look down.

Slightly under an hour into his walk, He saw the man and dog pass the big driftwood log he'd used as a reference point for locating the midden. He hoped the pair would either turn around and head back to their car sometime soon, or just keep walking.

He'd know the answer soon enough.

As he closed to within a couple of hundred metres, he picked up a stout driftwood branch he found just above the high tide mark to use as a walking stick. The stick didn't look like an obvious weapon, but would be good protection against dog attack in the event he needed it. He had his folding shovel attached to his daypack of course, but that was only half a meter long when fully extended. The branch, at just over two metres long, slightly taller than Sam and as thick as a softball bat, was a far better tool for fending off a dog should he need to.

He wondered if he was being paranoid. What was it about the man that made him think that he needed protection? He wasn't quite sure, but he'd learned to trust his gut.

Less than a hundred metres past the log, the man stopped and whistled to the dog. Sam could just make out the shrill sound over the tumble of the waves. He could tell something was about to happen, so he stopped. He moved up the beach a little and crouched down, trying to put the driftwood log between them. When the dog re-appeared from the scrub above the beach, Sam could see that he'd been right about it being a German shepherd. From the size of it, he wondered if the owner had been feeding it steroids. Its massive black and brown body must have weighed fifty kilos.

When the man led the dog inland near where Sam estimated

the midden to be, his heart sunk. What should he do? He didn't want to confront a man with a dog big enough to cause him a major injury, but neither did he want the man to find the midden and feel he had some claim to it.

Sam stepped from behind the log and walked slowly up the beach, acting like a typical jade hunter out for a walk. Meanwhile, he kept a close eye out for any sign of the pairs' return.

When he got to the spot where the pair turned inland, he was relieved to find himself still 20 metres short of the midden. He trudged up the slope following the line of footprints until they disappeared in the coarser shingle at the top of the beach. When he neared the first flax bush, he peeked over its protective foliage and tried to spot where the man and dog had gone.

At first glance Sam couldn't see them. Then, he saw the pair emerge from behind a clump of gorse a couple of hundred metres inland. Now, the man had the dog on a leash, while his other hand held what looked to be a shovel.

He watched as the man dug for a while. Ten minutes later, the two walked south for 100 meters before stopping and repeating the action.

As he watched, Sam wondered what the man was searching for. Was he looking for old gold mining equipment or relics of some sort? What else could be up there that would spark such interest?

He could be looking for jade, but it was unlikely. The area was a swampy river flat, and although strewn with rocks of all sorts, Sam doubted there'd be any jade lying about. It would have made far more sense to look for jade on the beach, rather than digging around in the scrub and gorse. Sam's eyes narrowed and his brow creased as he tried to figure out the puzzle.

After half an hour or so, the man moved away and turned back towards the beach further to the south. Sam figured it was safe for him to go back to the midden and get to work now they'd gone, but first he wanted to see what the man had been digging at.

Using the clump of gorse and another small tree behind it as a landmark, he walked towards the spot where the man and dog had been. Once past the gorse, he scanned left and right, then back again, as he walked.

Ten metres further on he stopped. There at his feet, freshly scraped into the sandy ground, lay a shallow depression in the shape of a grave.

A lump filled his throat.

What the hell is this guy doing?

The man had piled earth and rock to one side of the hole up to the level of his shins. Familiar looking boot prints were clearly visible in the bottom of the hole.

A piece of bone lying on the ground near the heap caught his attention. He bent down to examine it further but quickly realised it was the rib of a sheep or goat, and left it where it lay.

More confused than ever, Sam retraced his tracks back to the beach. He looked south, towards where the man and dog had been heading, but there was no sign of them. As far as his eyes could see, the beach was empty. He shrugged, figuring the pair must have rounded the point.

Pleased to have the place to himself again, Sam walked back down to the beach. Once on the sand, he turned north and walked past the spot where he'd disguised the midden. 50 metres beyond it, he turned and walked up onto the shingle bank and then doubled back along the scrub line. This way, if someone came along while he was working, or if the man with the dog returned, his location wouldn't be as obvious as it would have been had he left a trail of prints directly to the midden from the beach.

If he checked the beach every ten minutes or so, he reckoned he'd have plenty of time to duck down behind a clump of scrub if he spotted someone coming. Then, with any luck, they'd pass by without noticing he was there.

Once he reached the site, Sam smiled. Everything was just as he'd left it. Determined to be more methodical in his approach this time, he dropped his daypack to one side and undid the straps securing his shovel. After unfolding the head of the shovel and screwing the lock-nut into place, he started scraping a shallow trench around the perimeter of midden, trying to gauge its extent.

Digging the stony ground was heavy work, but at least most of rocks he came across were no larger than his fist. Around the edge of the midden the vast majority of the debris he was shifting was sand, shells, and lumps of burnt wood that looked almost like coal. Among the shells he occasionally found bird and fish bones.

A few times he stopped digging to have a closer look at a piece of rock, checking its edge for the telltale signs of it having been worked by man. One or two pieces he put into his daypack, ready for further investigation once he got back to the batch. He worked his way gradually inward, trying his best not to miss anything.

Every ten minutes or so, he checked the beach for visitors. Once, he saw what looked like people quite some distance off, but the sea-haze and sand whipped up by the rising wind made visibility difficult. In any case, whoever it was didn't seem to be heading in his direction.

Not long after he resumed work, he came across a scraper that had been knapped from a larger piece of rock. A series of small chips along the stone's edge gave a good indication the piece had been fashioned into a tool by someone.

After putting the suspected artefact into his daypack, he looked at his watch. It was 7:00 p.m. time to hide the signs of his activity as much as possible and head back to his car while he still had enough light, and before the tide was so high it made the return trip dangerous.

Sam hefted the daypack over his shoulder, and returned to the beach by the same circuitous route.

As he walked back towards his vehicle, he had time to watch the colourful sunset. A few dark clouds hugged the land further to the south, but out to sea, the sun shone in such a way that it gave the ocean a look of solidity, and made the clouds along the horizon look like islands or small hills protruding above an endless glistening plain.

As the colours deepened, Sam could almost imagine he was on a planet in some distant galaxy, looking across an alien landscape of red and orange protruding from a sea so incredibly blue it couldn't possibly be on earth. Slowly, the sun's flaming orb sunk lower and lower, until it flashed one last time and disappeared.

Before Sam knew it, he was back at his car. His was the only vehicle in the parking area. There was no sign of man or dog.

Sam took one last look to the southeast towards the high mountains. Silhouetted against them in the foreground, ancient rata, their branches outstretched like a sprinter's arms, appeared to be running along the river flats, as if racing from the fading light.

Chapter 7 - Wednesday Evening

Lydia set her paperback on the vanity, and turned on the hot tap to warm up her bath. Leaning back, she rested her head against the edge of the tub while considering the surprise ending to the book.

With her eyes closed, it didn't take much effort to imagine Sam McKee as the main character in the story — tall and strong, fighting the good fight against the forces of evil, frantically searching for two missing kids kidnapped by a psychopathic killer. Yes, if they ever turned the book into a movie, Sam would be perfect for the role.

The long soak had helped relieve the tension of the previous few days. As she lay there, she contemplated her situation. It hadn't been until Mr G had left for Auckland that she realised just how glad she'd been to see him go.

She wondered how she had allowed herself to become dependent on a man she didn't love. Why she'd let Mr G's wealth influence her decision to move in, rather than basing it on true affection. With 20/20 hindsight, it was all so clear.

She'd had an inkling she was making a mistake at the time, but she hadn't listened to her inner voice. Instead, she'd convinced herself it would be okay. That if things didn't work out she could leave any time she wanted. That it would only be until she got on her feet.

She buried her face in her hands and closed her eyes. Something had to change. Mr G treated her like a fool at work and a chattel at home.

After a few moments of self loathing, Lydia shook her head, gritted her teeth, and stood up. She reached for one of the towels hanging on the heated rail, patted her red eyes, and gave her hair a quick once over. After rubbing herself down, she twisted the towel around her head, and took the towelling robe off the hook on the back of the ensuite door and secured it around her waist

Taking the paperback, she made her way to the kitchen with

a cup of tea in mind. As she passed the sideboard, the phone shrilled. She dropped the book on the silver tray where she and Mr G usually left mail and their keys, to remind her to return it to the girlfriend who'd loaned it to her, and picked up the receiver.

"Hello?"

Nobody answered.

"Hello? Are you there?"

Lydia wondered who had called as she waited for the kettle to boil. She figured it was probably Mr G checking to see if she'd gone out. The same thing always happened when he was out of town. Didn't he realise she'd catch on?

"Stupid sod." If only he'd be more honest and straightforward. If only he could respect her and treat her as an equal, rather than playing silly games on the phone.

With cup in hand, she looked around her gilded cage with its granite benches, leather upholstery, and original art, and realised she needed to do some serious thinking about an exit strategy. This opulent display of wealth had impressed her at first, but what a fool she'd been. Mr G's new Mercedes, penthouse apartment, and Colin McCahon painting provided little comfort when he treated her like she was a possession too.

*****

When Sam reached the main road, he turned south toward the cottage. He felt good. He'd been down in this part of the country a number of times, but this was the first time he'd found a site with such promise. He'd only excavated half of the midden and already he'd found the patu, a scraper, as well as a few other pieces that might be artefacts. Add those to the jade pebble he'd found on the beach earlier in the day, and it made quite a haul. Especially considering in past years he'd gone days at a time without finding anything at all.

As he drove, his mind returned to the shallow hole he'd found, and what the man with the dog might be up to. Was the man planning to bury something, or was he looking for something? It seemed a strange place to do either.

Maybe the man was a bottle collector looking for the remains of some old homestead. Sam was sure he'd seen historic photos of a small settlement down this way on the wall of the pub. Could he be looking for the camp of one of the various gold sands operations that had existed on the beach before the turn of the century? With the area's rich history, both were possibilities.

Sam also wondered what tomorrow would bring. Would there be more treasure, or would he just end up with more puzzles to solve?

Ten minutes or so after rejoining the main highway he saw a sign designating the small settlement of Barrytown, population 225, situated a few miles north of his rented accommodation. As he neared the intersection, a white truck pulled out of the village's main street and passed him going in the opposite direction.

From front-on, Sam didn't recognise the truck as the one parked at the end of Burke Road when he'd arrived that afternoon. However, as the two vehicles passed each other, he caught sight of a huge German shepherd sitting in a cage on the back of the truck.

Sam slowed and stared into his rear vision mirror, but apart from the arse end of a rapidly disappearing dog there wasn't much to see.

Intrigued, he decided to stop off at the pub to celebrate his good fortune with a beer and a burger. He would also see if he could gather some information about the truck's owner.

When he pulled into the pub's car park, it was half-full. There were a couple of short wheel base 4x4s, favoured by the local landowners, cars in various states of repair, a camper van, and a small tour bus run by the backpackers accommodation attached to the pub.

Some of the patrons were drinking on the veranda where they were allowed to smoke. It was a great spot, with a clear view across the flats down to the coast about a kilometre away. Sam had sat there a few times on previous trips, to watch the sunset.

As he climbed the three steps up to the veranda, he nodded towards a couple of familiar faces before heading into the bar to order. Inside, a few local farmers were gathered at the near end of the bar drinking jugs of draught beer and munching on the free peanuts Ronnie, the pub's owner, supplied.

Sam caught the publican's attention and smiled. He found it difficult not to smile when he saw Ronnie. Ronnie had curly tuffs of the brightest red hair Sam had ever seen. He hadn't been surprised when he'd been told Ronnie had been teased, and called Ronald McDonald as a child. It must have been tough with that strawberry mop of hair. Still, Ronnie had done well for himself. He now owned the pub, a dozen accommodation units, not to mention a thriving bottle shop and family style restaurant.

As Ronnie gave Sam his pint, Sam leaned forward so publican could hear him over the surrounding conversations and laughter. "So who's the guy with the monster German shepherd I saw leaving?"

"I don't really know," Ronnie replied. "He's come in a couple of times, but only ever has one beer. Doesn't want to leave his dog too long he says."

"Not local then."

"No, but I'm sure I know his face from somewhere, but buggered if I can remember where."

"What's he like?"

"He's an odd one, that's for sure. Preoccupied I'd call it. Doesn't really talk much, just sits at the table by the window, has a beer, then pisses off."

Discouraged at the lack of information, Sam took his beer to the table he assumed the dog owner would have sat at, and waited for his burger.

From the window he had a view of the pub's car park, which made sense if the man wanted to watch his dog. It also gave a good view down into the village and the half-dozen or so houses that lined the street. Outside one of the houses, a group of teenagers gathered, hands in pockets, their bicycles lying in a bunch on the front lawn as they talked.

Directly across the road from the pub was an old wooden building, dilapidated and falling apart, typical of many along the West Coast. The faded sign on its front said something about engineering, but the paint had flaked to an extent that the lettering was illegible in the gloom. A rusty old tractor and what looked like a hay-baler stood abandoned in the small yard to the side of the building. A single streetlight flickered.

While deep in thought, Sam's meal arrived. He looked around and realised only himself and a couple that looked the likely owners of the camper van were eating. No wonder the burger came so quickly.

Friday nights would be a different story, but it suited Sam the place being quiet. He could almost hear the cogs turning in his skull.

As he ate, he thought back to the previous Saturday night, and the poker game that had funded this quick jaunt south. He wouldn't need to work for three months or so thanks to the unexpected windfall.

When Mr G invited him to the poker game on the day he'd gone to collect his money for recovering the Mercedes, his gut told him to steer clear, and that Mr G was trouble. Did he really want to get further involved in this man's world?

Despite his reservations, he was tempted. Curiosity made him wonder why the brothel owner had invited someone who was essentially an employee, to play cards with him and his 'good mates' as he'd described them.

There were lots reason not to accept the invitation, but on the plus side of the ledger, there was the possibility of more work, and the chance he might see Lydia again.

He didn't have a regular poker school going at that time, and Wellington didn't have a casino. So, despite his better judgement, he went along, planning to keep a low profile, play a tight game, and see what happened. If he could make a few dollars without ruffling too many feathers, who was he to complain? If things turned to custard, he'd walk away and never go back.

It didn't take Sam long to realise the only reason he'd been invited to join the game was to make up the numbers. That, and Mr G's egotistical belief that his poker prowess would allow him to win back some of the money he'd paid Sam for recovering his car.

Most of Mr G's mates were fish when it came to playing cards, so maybe he expected Sam to slot into the same category. If he'd taken the time to research who he was dealing with, as Sam had done, he might have played things differently.

Mr G might have found out that Sam had been involved in a number of big cash games over the years, and often came out on top. He might have discovered that Sam's study of odds and probability was well known in gambling circles, and that Sam's father had lived and played as a pro in Las Vegas for a number of years prior to his death from cancer. More importantly, Mr G might have discovered that the poker pro had passed on a fair bit of his knowledge to his son.

Sam tipped his beer and chuckled at his good fortune. "Cheers for the holiday, Mr G."

*****

When Mr G finished his shower, he dressed in silk boxers, a crisp white business shirt, and a light-weight wool suit. He put on merino socks, Italian loafers, and to finish, slipped his gold Rolex onto his wrist.

Before heading down to the restaurant, he rummaged through one of the interior pockets of his suitcase and pulled a slim, six-inch blade, out from under his cell phone charger. With a practised flick of his wrist, the weighted blade snapped open ready for use. He grinned, waving the razor-sharp steel in front of his face, before pushing a button on the side of the knife's handle that allowed him to fold the blade away.

He took one last look in the mirror and tweaked the knot of his tie. "That's better," he said to his reflection.

Now that he was looking smart and had his trusty knife in his pocket, he felt ready to do some business.

He was the only one in the lift as it descended to the second-floor restaurant where he requested a secluded table in the back where he could think.

After a light meal of salmon and salad, he ordered a large brandy and a short black coffee to finish. When his coffee arrived, he phoned Jimmy. "I'll be out front in ten minutes."

"Sure thing, Mr G. I'm travelling."

Mr G only had a minute to wait before Jimmy pulled his car in under the canopy outside the front door of the hotel. He walked briskly across the foyer, through the door, and climbed into the back.

Jimmy was still dressed in his dark suit, but he'd lost the chauffeurs cap. He was now in muscle mode. Ready to do whatever job Mr G needed. Not that Mr G needed much backup.

"First stop Queen Street. You know my establishment there don't you, Jimmy?"

"No worries, Mr G ... Should only take fifteen minutes' tops."

"Well, off we go then."

Mr G used Jimmy for odd jobs whenever he was in Auckland, and found him reliable in a 'do what you're told' sort of way. He liked it that Jimmy didn't ask questions or try to second guess what he wanted. Jimmy was a follower, a part-time private in Mr G's personal army. Their arrangement was uncomplicated. Mr G paid Jimmy an excellent hourly rate for his labour and use of the car, and Jimmy's job description included whatever Mr G wanted it to.

When he wasn't working for Mr G, Jimmy drove corporate clients. It was an arrangement that worked just fine for the both of them.

After he pulled to the curb in front of a three-storied turn of the century building on lower Queen Street, Jimmy got out and opened the car door for Mr G and then followed his boss into the building's small lobby.

Once in the lobby, clients would normally ring a doorbell to gain admission to the brothel proper. Mr G didn't ring the bell.

Instead, he slotted a key into a brass lock, turned the key, and pushed.

The door opened into a short hallway which led on to a large lounge with plush red carpet and decor right out of the twenties. A number of high-backed leather chairs and settees were lit from above with intricate glass chandeliers. Gilt mirrors and picture frames adorned the walls. A huge faux-marble fireplace, complete with brass candlesticks at each end, graced the wall to the left, and a small upholstered bar, with matching leather stools, occupied a secluded area to the right.

Past the bar, a wooden door with a reinforced glass window flanked by two potted palms stood slightly ajar. Below the window was a brass plaque with the word 'manager' engraved on it.

Draped on chairs and settees around the room, were woman in various stages of undress. Jimmy's eyes darted around, taking in the scene, but Mr G barely looked at the half-naked women. Instead, his focus was on the manager's office.

As the two men walked across the room, the girls remained lethargic, reacting as if the men weren't there, saving their smiles for paying customers.

Mr G turned to Jimmy. "Make sure no one comes in. Ethan and I need to sort out a few management issues."

Jimmy nodded, and pulled the door open for Mr G, before placing his back to it and crossing his arms.

In the office, a small man with a fine wisp of a beard sat behind the desk, scribbling furiously into a ledger. He looked up when the door banged shut just in time to see Mr G pull down the blind.

Ethan stopped writing and stood up. "Mr G, I can explain."

"What makes you think I give a shit for your lame excuses?"

"But, Mr G, I've … I've been working hard for you."

"If you call lining your own pocket while the girls run riot then yes, you've been working very hard sunshine."

"I'm not stealing from you, Mr G, I swear. Why would I do that?"

"Okay, let's have a gander at the books then. I'll know soon enough if you're lying."

"Sure, Mr G, here have a look. I'm just updating them for you."

Ethan resumed his seat and began leafing through the ledger. "As you can see here, takings are up 6% over the same month last year."

Mr G walked around behind Ethan's chair, and placed one hand on the manager's arm as if to read the ledger over his shoulder. His other hand retrieved the knife from his pocket.

Mr G's arm flashed around Ethan's neck, tightened under his chin, forcing Ethan's head back and up. With a quick flick, the knife snapped open.

Ethan gasped when the blade appeared inches from his face. He started to struggle but Mr G tightened his grip, cutting off Ethan's air supply to the point where his eyes started to bulge.

"Do you think I'm stupid you rat-faced bastard?" Mr G growled into Ethan's ear.

"No, no, Mr G, of course I don't th—think you're stupid," Ethan squeaked. "Owww! Please, let me go. I'll show you."

Mr G moved the knife away from Ethan's face, pointing it towards the ceiling. "Let me show you something, Mr Shit-For-Brains. See that light fitting up there?" Mr G twisted Ethan's head upwards. "Do you see it?"

As Mr G eased the pressure on Ethan's neck a little, Ethan blinked and tried to focus. "Yeah, yeah, I see it."

"Well that's where the camera is. You didn't think I'd let you run my place without supervision did you?"

"Please, Mr G. I can pay the money back. I swear I can pay it back!"

Sweat dripped off Ethan's reddening face and fell onto the pages of the ledger, smudging the ink. Mr G looked down at the mess in disgust.

"You think that's enough, you ferret-faced little fuck? You think you can steal from me, and then everything's going to be hunky-dory when you give me back what's already mine? I'd rather slit your scrawny throat."

"Mr G, I'll—I'll pay you back with interest. I'll give you

whatever you want. Please, please don't kill me."

"You'll pay interest alright, you ungrateful thief." Mr G inched the knife closer to Ethan's face. "You'll pay back what you owe, plus penalty interest of 50%."

"No problem, Mr G. Whatever you say."

Mr G sneered. "And secondly," he said tightening his grip on Ethan's neck once more and pressing the tip of the blade into the soft flesh of Ethan's cheek. "I'll have to leave you with a little something to remind you not to make the same mistake again. That's okay with you ... isn't it, Ethan?"

Chapter 8 - Thursday Morning

When the sun's rays fell across her bed, Lydia opened her eyes a crack and stretched her arms and legs. Rolling onto her side, she pulled the sheet up over her head and tried to go back to sleep, but it only took a few minutes before she gave up and tossed the duvet back.

She slipped on her robe and slippers, and padded her way to the kitchen where she made a cup of coffee. Sitting in her favourite chair, she surveyed the harbour while enjoying the strong Jamaican brew.

Cunard's *Queen Elizabeth* had arrived during the night, its towering superstructure dwarfing the containers stacked five-high at the wharf opposite and making the Interisland Ferry berthed nearby look like a toy.

As Lydia watched the activity on the water, she played with the idea of staying home. She was up to date with her work, and without Mr G being in town to order her about, what was the point? If she went into the office, she'd be bored by lunchtime.

Instead, she decided to take the morning off to get her hair done. Afterwards, she'd make a brief stop at the office to clear the mail, and then catch an afternoon movie.

The sound of the phone ringing dragged her back to the present. She hoped it wouldn't be Mr G wanting something. She put her cup on the side table and made her way towards the shrill buzzing.

"Hello?"

"It's me. I've decided to stay one more night, but I want you to book me on the 9:00 a.m. flight back to Wellington tomorrow morning."

"Anything else?"

"Yes, as soon as you get to work, I need you to go into my office and grab a phone number for me. It's on a post-it note tucked under the edge of my desk pad."

"Aren't they in the phonebook?" Lydia said, raising her eyes to the ceiling.

"No he's not in the bloody phonebook. This guy doesn't do phonebooks."

"But I was going to get my hair done this morning."

"Jesus woman, I'm not paying you to go to the hairdresser. Now do as I say. I may have a few other jobs for you as well. If you really need to get your hair done, do it this afternoon."

Lydia puffed air out her lips, made a face at the receiver, and hung up. Resigned about having to go to work, she poured herself a bowl of muesli and a second cup of coffee, and then had a quick shower.

On her way to the office, she stopped and bought a newspaper. Once at Graeme Developments, she sat her laptop on the reception desk, turned it on, and went into Mr G's office to find the number he wanted.

Under the edge of the burnished leather desk pad, sat a small slip of yellow paper. Lydia grabbed the note between her fingers and pulled, but as she did so, it slipped free and fluttered down under the desk.

"Damn it." Lydia said, climbing down onto her knees. "Come here you little bugger."

The phone number had drifted quite a way under desk, so as Lydia stretched her left arm out towards it, she twisted her head and shoulder back to increase her reach. Just as her fingers regained hold of the yellow square, she noticed a business card attached to the underside of the Mr G's desk with clear tape.

With the phone number safely in her grasp, Lydia swivelled around and tilted her head back so she could get a better look at the card. On it, written in small block letters were the characters AF-344-YT-6332

Lydia wondered what it was. Then it clicked. It must be a password of some sort, but for what?

After memorising the password, she returned to her desk and wrote it down on a fresh sheet of paper. Then, she folded the paper a number of times, and slipped it into her purse.

Dropping into her chair, Lydia caressed her temples with

her thumb and middle finger as she tried to figure out what the series of numbers and letters could possibly mean.

This group of characters were nothing like his normal passwords, which usually related to his obsession with Mercedes Benz cars. She'd seen him type his email password once when he didn't realise she was watching. That had been MyMercedes69, and the companies alarm code was Merc2010. This password was something else all together, a combination to a safety deposit box or a safe perhaps.

A few minutes later she realised she'd forgotten to call Mr G.

"Here's that number you wanted."

"It's about bloody time," he said, grabbing a pen to write it down. "Now don't forget to book that flight. Leave the details with reception here at the hotel, and I'll see you tomorrow morning."

"Do you want me to pick you up?"

"Nah, I'll catch a cab. I've got a couple of errands to run before I come in."

After they'd finished, Lydia hung up the phone and rang Air New Zealand.

"What's the least reliable aircraft you've got?" she asked the ticket seller.

"Excuse me madam?"

*****

Sam slept more soundly on the West Coast than he ever did in Wellington. He figured it was the peace and quiet combined with the increase in exercise he got while jade hunting. In any case, he awoke with a clear head and renewed excitement in getting back to the midden.

Low tide was an hour later today, which made his departure less urgent than it had been the previous morning. He leaned back in the chair, crossed his legs on the edge of the table, and watched the waves roll in from across the Tasman as he drank his morning cuppa and ate his muesli.

The grey clouds offshore were moving closer to the coast.

Dark streaks of rain, illuminated by the pale morning light, told him he was more likely to need wet-weather gear than sunscreen for his walk today.

After finishing breakfast and packing his daypack, he jumped into the Toyota and drove north towards Burke Road. Once past the pub, he slowed down and started looking for the dog owner's truck at the various properties he passed along the way. Whenever he saw a glimpse of white down a driveway, he slowed even more.

His interest in the man didn't surprise him. After years of surveillance, he was used to noticing things that seemed out of place, or not quite as they should be. There was something about this man that just didn't add up. A niggling curiosity had started to creep into his mind a little too often, and he wondered why. What had his subconscious picked up that his rational brain hadn't?

Shortly after Sam passed a large barn a couple of kilometres south of the Burke Road turnoff, he saw the white truck with its distinctive cage on the back, parked down a driveway. He slowed as he drove by, but saw no sign of the man or the dog.

Beyond the truck, an overgrown path led to a small cottage tucked away in a grove of beech trees. A faded sign out front advertised the cottage's availability for rent by the night, or the week, a common sight in the district over the late spring and summer period. Once he'd driven past the driveway, a solid wall of flax and other shrubbery blocked his view back to the house.

After checking his rear vision mirror, Sam pulled onto the shoulder. The publican had been right about the man not being local.

He debated turning the Toyota around and cruising past the driveway a second time, but figured if he wanted a decent look he'd need to get closer. But where was the dog? Should he risk exposing himself away from the safety of his vehicle?

After a moment's hesitation, Sam put the Toyota in gear and pulled as far off the road as possible, nestling the passenger side into the shrubbery before getting out. Carrying the folding shovel loosely in his right hand, he crept back towards the driveway.

Staying on the edge of the bitumen to avoid crunching the gravel that littered the side of the road, he peered through the roadside greenery as he went. Maybe he could find a spot that would allow him a view of the cottage without the need to expose himself at the property's entrance.

Twenty metres from his car, he noticed a gap in the bush and made his way across the shoulder. He stepped over a small drainage ditch, careful not to snap any of the dried branches lying on the other side. Pulling back the foliage as he went, he slowly worked his way into the greenery for a better look.

Tucked back in the trees, much of the house was hidden from Sam's view, but he had a good view of the truck. Next to the cage on deck, lay a long handled shovel and a length of rope.

He scanned the area around the cottage, but there was still no sign of man or his dog.

After watching for a few minutes, Sam couldn't see much point in hanging around any longer. At least now he knew where the man was staying. Unless he was prepared to walk up and knock on the door, pretending to be a Jehovah Witness or something, he didn't see much likelihood of finding out anything more by standing in the bush wasting good jade hunting time.

Just as Sam turned to head back to his vehicle, a door slammed.

Swivelling his head towards the cottage, Sam caught a flash of colour. The man had exited the cottage and was walking up the driveway. Sam figured he'd better scarper before he got caught spying. Then he noticed the gun in the man's hand.

When the dog barked, he wasted no time getting back to the Toyota. Tossing the shovel in the back seat, he jumped behind the wheel. He waited briefly for a milk tanker to thunder by the cottage in the hopes it would mask the sound of his vehicle starting, then threw gearshift into drive, and stomped on the accelerator.

*****

As the man stooped to load more wood into the wheelbarrow, he heard a vehicle slow and stop less than a hundred metres up the highway. He couldn't think of a good reason for someone to stop on this section of the highway. There were no driveways, lay-bys, points of interest, or scenic lookouts for a couple of kilometres. This section of the Coast Road ran nearly straight until it passed Burke Road. Only then did it begin to wind its way up the hill towards the village of Punakaki.

The man, suspicious by nature, and thinking some dishonest local might be checking the place out to see if there was anything worth stealing, looked down at the dog who'd wandered out to keep him company.

"Down Brutus ... quiet."

Brutus dropped to the ground, his tail twitching, alert for his master's next command. As the dog waited, the man crept back to the house and slipped in through the back door. He removed the shotgun hidden under his bed, and slotted two rounds of birdshot into the chambers.

"Heel Brutus," he said, rushing out the front door ready to confront the stranger. As the man marched down the drive towards the road the dog leapt to his feet and barked.

Just as they reached the main road, a milk tanker whooshed by heading south. The man threw up a hand to shield his eyes from the cloud of grit blown up by the tanker's wheels. As the dust settled, he looked to the north and saw the Toyota accelerating down the highway a puff of black smoke belching from its exhaust.

The vehicle looked similar to the one he'd seen parked at the end of Burke Road the previous day when he came back from the river flats. The spare wheel cover on its rear certainly looked the same. 'Back Off' it said. How many of those could there be?

The last thing he wanted was for people to know what he was up to. Some nosey local getting wind of his plans would spoil everything.

The man scratched his head, and meandered back down the drive towards the cottage, unloading the shotgun as he went. Brutus, as always, followed close behind.

After putting the shotgun away, the man went back to the woodshed to finish loading the wheelbarrow. He wheeled it up to the front porch, and grabbed a couple of hunks of wood off the top of the pile to feed the fire.

For many people, having to light a fire to heat hot water would be a hassle, but he liked mucking around with fire. He liked chopping the larger rounds of wood into manageable wedges, the weight of the axe in his hands as he powered down through the wood, splitting it into smaller pieces.

Normally, he would have had hot water left over from the previous night, but he'd drawn a huge bath, and once the water had cooled he'd emptied some water out and refilled it with more hot. The long bath had given him plenty of time to think about how he'd handle things once he found the girl.

As the fire roared, hot water in the wetback circulated up through the copper pipes, and entered the hot-water cylinder. Within half an hour, he had enough steaming water to do the breakfast dishes, have a wash, and shave the stubble off his face.

Brutus was happy to bask in the warm glow of the wood burner while the man went though his morning routine. The heat eased the ache in the old dog's joints, and within a few minutes, he had nodded off to sleep.

A whistle from the man brought an abrupt halt to the dog's dreaming. Brutus climbed to his feet, and gave his body a brief shake, before following the man out of the house, down the steps, and onto the back of the truck.

*****

As he drove, Sam reminded himself that having a firearm didn't mean the man was out to do something sinister. Most likely, he'd be off to do a bit of hunting. It was the West Coast after all. Lots of people came here to shoot deer and pigs. Maybe he planned some target shooting down at the gun club in the village. Both were possibilities. Despite this logic, Sam's niggling doubts about the man and his motives refused to leave. The hole he'd found the previous day, certainly didn't help in that regard. What sane person went around digging graves in the middle of nowhere?

Sam considered doubling back to follow the man and see where he went, but decided it was better to mind his own business and get back to the midden. His Toyota would be far too obvious on this section of the Coast Road anyway. And what would happen if the man realised he was being followed? Would he get angry? A monster dog owner, with a gun, getting angry at him, was the last thing he needed.

Sam didn't have far to drive before the Burke Road turnoff loomed up on the left. He pulled onto the gravel road, dodging potholes and pukekos as he made his way towards the parking area.

At the end of the road, the occupants of a camper van were in the process of packing their gear up. They were the only people Sam saw as he parked in his usual spot.

Sam grabbed his daypack, folding shovel, oilskin, and wide-brimmed hat from the back seat and locked up the Toyota. He nodded to the young couple as he started across the stream towards the beach.

The pair of tourists looked quizzically at Sam, pointing at the charcoal-grey clouds and sweeping bands of rain heading in their direction, before saying something in German that he figured could only be a warning. Sam just smiled and gave them the thumbs up, leaving the couple with amused looks on their faces as he splashed into the creek.

Rain fell lightly at first, but by the time Sam crossed the first creek, still 45 minutes from the midden, droplets large enough to create mini craters were thwacking down into the sand. He quickly donned his heavy oilskin, turned up its collar, and tied his rain hat securely under his chin to stop it from flying off in the ever increasing gusts of wind.

Within minutes, a solid grey curtain had come down, cutting him off from the world around him. The native bush on the hills to his right, clearly visible only moments before, had disappeared completely, and the huge Matai trees, a couple of hundred meters inland, had been transformed into eerie shapes that looked like strange extraterrestrial beings in the deepening mist and driving rain.

When the main storm front hit, the sound of the rain thrumming on the sand, overwhelmed that of the waves surging up and down the beach. Amid the cacophony of sound, Sam plodded on towards the midden. The worse the weather got, the more Sam grinned. He loved it when nature showed its power.

"Yahoooooooo!" he roared. "Do your worst big momma!"

Further up the shingle bank, wind-lashed flaxes and grasses danced frenetically in the murk. Sam shifted his upper body forward, trying to lower his profile to the gusts sweeping in from the sea. He walked forward, his left hand clutching the front of his oilskin, shoulder down into the gale for a hundred metres or so, but just as he found a balance between his forward angle and the intensity of the wind, the weather eased.

"Is that all you've got?"

By the time Sam neared the midden, the storm clouds had moved well inland, and the sun was starting to pierce its way through the clouds. Even the odd patch of blue sky had appeared. Before long, the hills took shape through the mist. As the sun's rays hit the beach, wisps of vapour began to rise off the slowly heating stones.

Sam, following the same procedure as the previous day, walked 50 meters past the midden before climbing up to the top of the shingle bank and doubling back. When he got there, he draped his oilskin and hat over a bush a few metres away to dry and started digging where he'd left off the day before.

*****

Mr G was startled awake by the sound of someone moving

around his hotel room, but then lowered his head back onto the pillow when he remembered the girl he'd brought home after dealing with Ethan.

When the tip of the knife sliced down his cheek from just below his eye, to the corner of his mouth, Ethan had not only bled like a pig, he'd squealed like one too. Not that the cut had been all that deep. Nonetheless, blood had soaked through a thick towel to the point where Mr G thought he might have to drop Ethan at the emergency department, with threats of murder if he told police what had happened.

Jimmy had come to the rescue by borrowing a sewing kit from one of the girls, and using his medical corps training to stitch Ethan's skin together and staunch the flow of blood. The end result wasn't pretty, but Mr G didn't care about that. He wanted Ethan, and everyone else who worked for him, to have a vivid reminder of what happened to people who stole from him.

When the toilet flushed, and the girl padded back to bed, Mr G closed his eyes again and tried to sleep. He had a couple of appointments later that morning, but after all the drama of the previous night, he just wanted to sleep.

Chapter 9 - Thursday Afternoon

Within two hours, Sam had a small pile of interesting objects. Whoever had occupied this site must have left in a hurry. He couldn't imagine earlier inhabitants leaving such items behind intentionally. They were too valuable, and would have taken their owners time and effort to replace.

As he lined the items up beside his daypack, he couldn't help but smile at all the booty; a small stone adze, some bird bone needles, another small scraper, not to mention a partially worked piece of greenstone in the shape of a tiki. It was an amazing haul for a morning's work. Had someone told him before leaving Wellington that he'd find so many different pieces in a single day, he would have laughed. But here they were, right in front of him.

Sam stood tall and looked around. He'd been lucky so far. The heavy rain, earlier on, had kept others off the beach. When he looked out to sea, another front was moving in. This one looked even nastier than the previous one. When he saw a bolt of lightning flash amongst its dark clouds, he knew it was time to head back to his vehicle. Besides, the tide was on the turn and would be racing in again before long.

If he had time at some stage, he might come back and scrape around in the general vicinity to check that nothing else had been dropped in haste, but for the moment, he was more than satisfied with his haul.

As the rain-laden clouds moved steadily closer, he packed everything into his bag as quickly as possible. Another flash of lightning crackled down in the distance, and a bone-rattling boom of thunder followed eight seconds later. The storm was close. Sound travels at a fraction under 350 metres per second, which made the front just over two kilometres away by Sam's calculations.

He had one last look around to make sure he hadn't left anything behind, and high-tailed it down to the beach, walking quickly towards the car park.

About halfway back to his car, he noticed dog prints in the sand. Prints that size could only belong to one dog that he knew.

This explained why Sam hadn't seen the man during his stints on lookout. He'd been further down the beach. Maybe the man had decided to stay closer to his truck because of the rain. Or maybe whatever activity he'd been engaged in didn't require a long walk today. It all just got stranger and stranger as far as Sam was concerned. Most people wouldn't even venture out on a day like today unless they had good reason.

As Sam rounded the last little headland, less than a kilometre from his vehicle, he saw a figure near the creek below the car park. There was no sign of any dog, nor did it look as though the person on the beach was wearing a backpack like the dog's owner often did.

As he closed in on the lone figure, he saw a flash of red hair poking out from under a wool beanie. It was Ronnie out for a jade hunt.

Sam waved and yelled out. "Any luck mate?"

Ronnie shook his head as he walked towards Sam. "Nah, nothing. You?"

"Nothing," Sam lied. "I got a wee pebble yesterday up near the first creek, but today's been a total waste of effort."

"Oh by the way, I saw that guy with the dog again." Ronnie said. "He was up on the flats. I thought he was out shooting rabbits at first, but then I noticed he was carrying a shovel."

"He was digging around down past the second creek yesterday too. I can't imagine what he expects to find on the flats way the hell down there."

Ronnie looked puzzled. "Past the second creek eh?

"You don't remember there being an old homestead or something down that way when you were a kid do you? Maybe he's looking for bottles or something like that. I noticed he dug a shallow hole just up from where an old creek bed runs towards the road. If it had been any deeper I'd have sworn the guy was digging a grave."

Ronnie's brow creased as he pondered what Sam had said.

"There are some odd people down this way. Loners, stoners, drifters, you name it. I see all types in the pub. The dude could be doing most anything and it wouldn't surprise me."

As the two men talked, the wind started to gust, and big drops of rain began pelting down. Sam and Ronnie both looked out to sea as another flash of lightning lit up the sky, followed less than a second later, by the boom of thunder.

"Shit that was close. Time to get moving I think," Sam said, turning to head back to his vehicle.

"Not wrong there mate."

Sam started the Toyota and did a quick U-turn before splashing and weaving his way back to the main road. On the drive back to his accommodation, he slowed as he passed the dog owner's rented house. The white truck sat in the same spot as earlier, and smoke billowed from the chimney. It looked like the man was in for the duration. With the rain pounding down as it was, he doubted the man would be going anywhere, anytime soon.

*****

The man wrinkled his nose as he put another piece of wood on the fire. "Jesus, Brutus, you smell like wet socks."

Brutus opened his eyes, and looked up from his spot by the fire. He didn't know what his master had said, but he didn't sound angry so the dog closed his eyes and went back to sleep.

The man turned to where he'd put his pack, and started pulling his gear out. Grabbing a cloth he wiped down each item before putting it aside. He couldn't abide dirty equipment. Cleanliness was next to godliness. It was a lesson he'd learned as a child. His mother would roll in her grave if she'd seen the state of his gear.

After cleaning, disassembling, and restacking everything ready for the next day, the man went into the kitchen and put the kettle on. While he waited, he tidied up the dishes in the kitchen cupboard. The cups and plates were in such a mess. Unless they were straight, he felt uneasy.

With his tea in hand, he went back to where Brutus slept and poked at the fire a few times. Sitting down in the armchair, he leaned towards the fire, elbows on knees, and wrapped his hands around the mug as he stared at the flames visible through the glass door of the wood burner.

Opening and closing his hands a few times, the man stretched his fingers to get the circulation working properly. It had been a long wet morning on the flats, and his arthritis was giving him hell. They were a right pair the two of them, Brutus with his wonky hips, and him with his knotted fingers.

"We're getting old eh Brutus?"

The man hadn't expected to see the publican out on such a horrible day. Why would Ronnie bother with the weather being so horrible? Any sensible person would have stayed indoors.

The man scratched his head. Maybe today was the publican's only day off. He remembered overhearing some of the locals at the bar talking about how Ronnie searched the beach for jade whenever he had a chance. The pieces he had for sale in the display case in the bar were certainly testament to the miles he must have walked to find so many beautiful stones.

But even if Ronnie's reasons for being out on such a day were innocent, the man didn't like the idea that one of the locals might realise what he was up to. That could spoil his plans, and ruin all his careful planning. Months of preparation would go down the drain if the wrong person got wind of his plans.

He pulled the picture from his top pocket and looked at the girls face, as he did many times each day. She was thirteen years old and very pretty. Her long blond curls and blue eyes reminded him of his own daughter. Not that he'd ever see her again. No, he'd buried her almost five years ago.

After looking at the photo for a few minutes, the man put it back into his top pocket and leaned back in his chair thinking about his next step. He wondered how he'd feel if he found her, and if finding her would give him the peace he so desperately sought.

When he finished his tea, the man went and unpacked his gear once again just to double check everything was there. He'd hate to forget something important. He'd never forgive himself if he messed things up at this late stage.

*****

Lydia liked the feel of her new hair. With the split-ends trimmed off, and the special conditioning treatment she'd had done, it now bounced with life, sparkling in the sunlight as she walked. She caught her reflection in a shop window as she strolled down Manners Street towards her apartment, and smiled at what she saw.

Rush hour had just begun, and the streets were crowded. A gust of air blasted into her as a trolley bus whizzed past, a little too close for comfort. She'd read in the paper that morning that yet another pedestrian had been knocked over not far from where she was walking. Instinctively she moved further to her left, not wanting one of the many pedestrians crowding the footpath, to bump her into the street.

Before turning into Taranaki Street, she popped into her favourite Thai restaurant and ordered a Pad Thai to have for dinner. Inhaling deeply as she walked through the door, she filled her nostrils with the smell of lemongrass and chilli. Lydia loved cooking, but cooking for one didn't hold much appeal. Besides, she thought, with food like this available at her doorstep why bother.

As she waited for her order, she sat at a small table near the counter and leafed through a travel magazine. She'd had a great time in Europe with Mr G. The old buildings and the history were fascinating. The days she spent wandering the museums and galleries of London and Paris, while Mr G went to his business meetings, were some of her best ever.

It was early in their relationship and Mr G had been quite the charmer on the trip. He'd gotten grumpy a few times when things didn't go as well as he'd hoped with his business, but most days he was pleasant and left her to do whatever she wanted, rather than insist she accompany him.

The week in Paris had been her favourite. Their room was in a small boutique hotel in Montmartre, not far from the Sacre Coeur. In the mornings after Mr G left to go to his meetings, she would wander the narrow streets, drink cafe au lait, and eat croissants or pan chocolate in one of the many cafes. After lunch, she'd catch the subway into the city to visit sites like Notre Dame, Musee d'Orsay, and the Louvre.

In the evenings, they'd go out for a meal, drink the local wine, enjoy the warm nights, and listen to music. One night, much to Lydia's surprise, they even went dancing.

However, once they got back to Wellington, and she'd moved into his apartment, the relationship soured, with him reverting to type and becoming the brothel owner once more. Despite her efforts to recreate that wonderful week in Paris by cooking French food and buying special bottles of wine, she could feel the relationship spiralling further and further into one of servant and master.

When Lydia's food arrived, she dropped the magazine back on the stack and paid the young woman behind the counter. Carrying the small plastic bag with its steaming contents, she made her way home.

After entering the apartment, she tossed her purse on the table and her keys in the silver tray. She poured a glass of Sauvignon Blanc from a half-full bottle in the fridge, sat down at the table, and opened the steaming container of Pad Thai.

As she ate, more memories of Paris flooded her mind. If only she hadn't lost her savings when the finance company had crashed, she would have had enough money to say 'stuff it' and leave Mr G. She could have jumped on the first plane out of town and once again be in control of her destiny.

The photos in the magazine at the Thai restaurant had reminded her of those balmy nights having dinner at an outdoor cafe, the waiters having a friendly laugh at her attempts to speak French. The coq au vin, ratatouille, and other French cuisine she loved so much, and the wine – the delicious wine that flowed freely from every restaurant and cafe in the city.

She saw Paris as a happy place, full of vivacious and eclectic people. Exaggerated in their language and their expressions, but kind and not in the least arrogant like she'd expected, especially when they found out she wasn't British and came instead from New Zealand, home of the All Blacks rugby team.

She laughed when she remember immaculately dressed women, carrying tiny bejewelled dogs, in their Gucci handbags, as they shopped at Louis Vuitton, Cartier, and Chanel. Her naive eyes had been opened to a world of style, sophistication, grace, and charm.

If only she could find a way to escape back to such places.

Once she'd finished eating, Lydia poured a second glass of wine and took it to the chair by the window. The moon had begun to rise over the hills of the Miramar Peninsula, yellow and huge as it sat low in the sky, its golden rays adding to those created by the city lights reflected in the mirror-still water of the harbour.

The crisp cool wine, had given her a slight buzz. She curled her legs up and rested her head as she watched the scene out the window. Halfway through her second glass of wine, she remembered the password and went to grab it from her purse.

Unfolding the paper, she looked at the strange combinations of letters and numbers again wondering what AF-344-YT-6332 could possibly mean.

It had to be a combination of some sort, she figured. Passwords didn't have dashes between sets of characters. They must signify a combination in four parts.

She wondered what Mr G might keep in a safe if he had one. Would it be undeclared income from the brothels he ran? Gold or jewellery perhaps? Stocks and bonds? Her mind whirled with possibilities. Just the thought of finding the safe made her giddy. Whether she'd have the nerve to do anything with it once she did, was another matter. A slight tingle ran up her spine. She couldn't remember the last time she'd been so excited.

Maybe she should have a look around the apartment just for a laugh. Mr G would never know. Besides, finding out some of his secrets might come in handy one day.

Lydia put down her empty wine glass, and went to the bedroom to change into something more comfortable. Then she sat on the bed and tried to think logically. Where would she put a safe if she had one?

With its clean lines and open plan, the contemporary apartment didn't have a lot of hiding places. She got up from the bed and walked to the large double wardrobe that ran down one wall. Opening the door, she shifted the clothing on the hangers from side to side, finding nothing. She pulled out the wire baskets that held Mr G sweaters, socks and underwear, and looked at any wall areas where a safe might be hidden. She checked the floor under his shoe rack.

After searching the wardrobe, she rolled the bed out from the wall on its castors. Nothing, nor were any of the pictures in the bedroom to hide anything behind. The mirror over a built in vanity was fixed to the wall, so she pulled out the vanity's drawers, and checked the cavity behind them. Still nothing.

Sweating slightly from her exertions, she stood in the middle of the lounge and rotated slowly around as she surveyed the place for possible hiding places. When she saw nothing, she took a couple deep breaths through her nose, puffing the air out between her lips.

"Now think Lydia. Where would he put a safe?" she mumbled.

Behind the paintings was an obvious a place, but she doubted he'd be that predictable. Still, she checked anyway. She knew the large buffet didn't have anything behind it, because it had been moved closer to the poker table when the men had played cards the previous weekend. She'd even taken the opportunity to dust the skirting board behind where it normally sat at the time.

With arms folded across her chest, she did one more rotation, but nowhere in the room could she see a possible hiding place.

In the kitchen she searched the cupboards, behind the fridge, and in the pantry, she gave up and sat down at the table to rethink her strategy. As she pondered the situation, she looked across the room to the lounge once again.

Then it clicked.

"Of course!" She squealed, rubbing her hands together in front of her chest as she bounced excitedly in place.

In the corner of the lounge, stood a large model of a classic Mercedes, sitting on a polished block of black granite. The black granite contrasted the silver car, setting it off to perfection. At approximately 400mm long and 150mm wide, the model was Mr G's favourite possession. She remembered him telling her he'd had the pedestal custom made to display it.

Lydia crossed the room and peered at the model. All looked normal. She ran her fingers around the edges of the granite. The piece looked solid from a distance, but when she got right up close, she could see the thinnest of lines at the corners where the pieces of granite had been expertly joined, and another pair of joins about halfway down the front. It wasn't a solid block after all. The manufacturer had made it from pieces, and if that was the case, she figured they could come apart somehow, if only she could work out the mechanics of it all.

Looking closely at the car, she searched for signs of a switch or lever that might open a secret compartment, assuming there was one. She had to be careful. She didn't want to risk breaking Mr G's model. Mr G always bragged about how much he'd paid for it. She'd never hear the end of it were she to damage it in some way.

The model was solid silver, with crystal headlamps and diamond indicator lenses. Its designer was a famous German model-maker that Lydia felt she should remember the name of because of the number of times she'd heard Mr G tell the story, but cars didn't interest her. Normally she switched off whenever the topic came up. Anything to do with cars bored her rigid. She'd had enough about cars as a child. Her father had been a car enthusiast who'd spent more time restoring his

1940 Ford coupe, than he had with his children.

Every time Mr G told the story of how he'd found the model. How he'd flown to Germany to collect it, how much it had cost, and all the detail about the scale, the model number, its top speed, cc rating, her eyes would glaze over. She'd gotten into the habit of popping off to the loo whenever he launched into the story to save herself the agony of hearing it again, which seemed ironic to Lydia, because right at that moment, the car was, without a doubt, the most interesting item in the entire apartment.

She inspected it from all sides. Then she squatted down until she was at eye level with it, her face no more than a hand's width away. Nothing she could see looked even remotely like a latch, or button.

But then, when she bent even lower to look at the narrow gap under the model, she noticed a metal rod extending from the car's chassis, down into the top of the granite plinth.

"Is the whole car the lever?"

Her chest pounded as she carefully grabbed each end of the model. She hoped she wasn't making an awful mistake. Mr G would be so angry if she damaged his pride and joy.

Still, curiosity won out.

But which way should she turn the damn thing? And would she damage it if she turned it the wrong way? Would it be alarmed?

Then she thought of her days in Paris and her desire to return.

She wiped her hands on her track pants, and gripped each end of the car, gently twisting it in an anti-clockwise direction. At first it didn't seem as though the car was going to move, but then the slightest of squeaks sounded as the mechanism engaged. Lydia rotated her shoulders a little more, putting subtle pressure on the model, pulling the left side while pushing the right.

After another few millimetres, there was a discernible click. The front section of the granite pedestal whooshed open with a hydraulic hiss, revealing an electronic safe. In the centre of its stainless steel door, a small red LCD panel blinked 0000.

Her jaw dropped and eyes widened as she sank to her knees to examine her discovery more closely. It felt like a flock of sparrows were trying to escape from her chest, and her pulse throbbed at her temples.

Now that she knew the safe existed, dare she open it? If she crossed this line, would it turn her into someone as bad as the person she wished to escape? What were her real reasons? Did she really need to do this to get away from the situation she'd found herself in?

Lydia went back to table and sat for a few minutes, allowing herself time to calm down and think. She wouldn't be committing a crime by just opening the safe, not if she didn't actually steal something would she?

Lydia picked up the paper with the combination on it, and turned it around in her hand as she considered her options. She could just close the granite panel and pretend the whole thing never happened. Alternately, she could try the combination and see if it opened the safe. She knew the first option carried a lot less temptation. The safe could be full of boring old papers or items of little value. However, if it contained a great big pile of cash, it could be her ticket out, her ticket to a new life.

Holding the paper at arm's length Lydia stared at the numbers for ages. Then, having finally made a decision, she stood and crossed the room towards the model Mercedes.

She looked hard at the blinking panel on the front of the safe, trying to figure out how to input the combination. Below the four red 0's were rows of letters and numbers. One button had a small green dot in its centre.

She chewed on her bottom lip as she reached forward. Holding the paper in one hand, she pressed the A and F buttons and then the green dot with the other.

The safe beeped.

She put in the number 344, and hit the green button. Again the safe beeped.

"So far so good ... I think."

But what if she'd activated a silent alarm? A security

company could have already despatched a car to investigate for all she knew. Better not to think of such things. Besides she reasoned, if the safe was alarmed, the penthouse would have had some sort of alarm too, and if that were the case, she would have known about it.

She ran the back of her hand across her forehead, and then wiped the perspiration on the leg of her pants before putting in the next two letters and hitting the green button once again. There was no point in over thinking things. She'd made her decision. Trembling, she entered the last four numbers.

Nothing happened.

"What the ...?" She said, wondering what she'd done wrong.

Then realising she'd forgotten to hit the green button after the last entry, she reached forward, pushed the button, and took a big step back.

Three beeps sounded, and a second later, the safe clicked opened.

At the sight of the open door, Lydia's whole body began to shudder, both in fear and excitement. She dropped to her knees and peered into the dark interior of the metal box.

The safe had a single shelf dividing its interior into two equal sized compartments. On the top of the shelf, were three ring binders and a couple of manila folders. On the bottom shelf sat bundles of banknotes, and a black book about the size of a diary, held closed with a thick rubber band. On top of the book sat a small felt-covered box about 150mm long.

She couldn't believe her eyes when she saw the cash. So much money in neat little bundles, more money than she'd ever seen at one time apart from on TV. She couldn't resist touching one bundle, just to make sure it was real.

Careful not to disturb anything, just in case Mr G noticed, Lydia slipped one bundle off the pile and ruffled through it to estimate how much it contained. After a rough count, she calculated there were one hundred, $100 dollar notes per bundle. So, with there being twenty bundles that made it ...

"My god that's nearly a quarter of a million dollars!"

This stack of cash made the 30k she'd lost when the finance company went belly-up look like spare change. After replacing the money, insuring the bundle lined up with the others, she reached for the felt box.

The box was heavier than it first looked. In the end she grabbed the sides of the black book and slid the two items out together to make it easier to remove. Once out from under the shelf, Lydia grabbed the box and placed it on the carpet to have a closer look. When she lifted off its lid, the contents glimmered and glistened.

The box contained gold coins. She pulled one from the box. The coin had a Canadian maple leaf on it. She'd read about these coins but had never actually seen one in real life. She knew each coin was one ounce of 99.9% pure gold. At current values, she estimated the twenty coins to be worth around fifty thousand New Zealand dollars.

As pretty as they were, Lydia didn't look at the coins for long. Even with Mr G in Auckland, she felt the need to get everything back in the safe as quickly as possible. Her heart raced. A slick of perspiration had turned her skin clammy, and her breathing was ragged.

Despite the fear jangling her nerves, she took hold of the book and slid off the rubber band. Inside she found names, phone numbers, amounts, and notes on events ranging back a number of years. It didn't take long for her to realise that much of the information in this book related to illegal activity.

One page alone contained the names of three prominent men with dollar amounts noted beside them. One she recognised as a member of the planning authority.

She didn't need to be a genius to realise this information was dangerous, not only for those who the information referred too, but to anyone else who found out about it. Feeling soiled by what she'd read, Lydia replaced the rubber band and put the book and the box back in the safe. The ring binders she left where they were. She'd seen enough.

Once she was sure everything had been replaced as she'd found it, Lydia shut the door. When it clicked, the LED display returned to 0000. Then she carefully closed the granite panel. As she did so, the model rotated back to its original position.

"Phew."

Just as she stood, the phone shrilled. Her hands flashed to her chest, and she nearly jumped out of her skin. She exhaled slowly, trying to relax as she walked over to picked up the receiver.

"Hello?"

"What are you up to?" Mr G asked. "Behaving yourself I hope."

Chapter 10 - Friday Morning

Mr G's 9:00 a.m. flight to Wellington didn't arrive until 11:05 due to low fog delaying flights out of Auckland. His plane had sat on the tarmac for over an hour waiting for clearance to take off.

Mr G fumed as he walked down the concourse, through the terminal, down the stairs, and outside to where he could catch one of the many waiting taxis. If he hadn't been running late he would have stopped for something to eat, but now he couldn't afford the time.

By the time the taxi pulled up outside his associate's house, his stomach was rumbling like a pair of tennis shoes in a tumble dryer.

Mr G got out of the cab and turned to the driver. "Wait here I'll be back shortly."

As Mr G carried his bag up to the front door, he could see the shadow of a man standing behind the net curtains in the front bay window. He didn't bother to knock.

"You're late."

"Don't you bloody well start mate. I've had a shit of a morning. Fucking fog."

"But you collected the shipment okay?"

Mr G hoisted his bag onto a dining chair, unclipped the latches, and opened the top. From inside, he brought out a velvet box and placed it on the table.

The heavyset man smiled as he reached out to touch the box, stroking its velvet lid as if it were the skin of a lover. Gently, he lifted the lid to reveal a row of shiny gold coins.

Mr G watched his associate's eyes as he peered at the box's contents. "This is what your stolen jewellery looks like once it's nicely washed and polished. Twenty-five gold Mapleleafs ... I bet your previous fence didn't give you many of these."

"You're not wrong there, Mr G. So, no problem with the transportation? The hidden compartment in the Merc worked out okay?"

"Fucking godsend really. Some bastard pinched the bloody car from outside my Vivian Street club only minutes before Jimmy was due to pick it up for the drive to Auckland. Imagine if the stuff had been sitting in a bag in the boot. Luckily, I managed to steal the car back before the thieves had any idea there was a shit-pile of bling stashed in the side panel. That's why these beauties have been a little late getting back to us."

"Sounds like we were lucky … still, lots of things worse than a week's delay." The man reached down and pulled one of the coins out of the box. Holding it between his thumb and forefinger, he tilted it back and forth, watching as it reflected the light. "Ain't it lovely?"

"Nothing quite like gold to make a man feel all warm and fuzzy that's for sure." Mr G said. "Now don't forget to get that into your safe deposit box ASAP. You don't want some wanker stealing it."

"Ha!" the man said, patting Mr G on the shoulder. "Now wouldn't that be ironic."

Mr G left the man admiring his treasure and went back out to the waiting cab. After a second stop of similar duration, the cab pulled up outside Mr G's office building.

Lydia did her best to smile when Mr G entered. "How was the flight?"

"Late. It's been a shit of a morning. I've got some calls to make. Would you pop out and grab me some sandwiches and make some coffee, if I don't get something into my stomach soon I'm going to starve."

Lydia took off, pleased to have a chance to get out of the office. Ever since she'd found the safe, all she could think about was how to steal its contents and get away before Mr G found out. The previous night, she'd dreamed of Paris, of strolling down the Champs de Elysees, and along the banks of the Seine. She'd dreamed of places far away from Wellington and Mr G.

This morning however, in the clear light of day, as she'd watched the effects of the cool wind blowing across the harbour and creating little whitecaps that broke against the seawall of the container terminal, she knew that stealing the money would be the easy part. Getting away was another matter altogether.

"Can I take your order?" the woman in the cafe said.

Lydia bought two bacon-and-egg sandwiches, and walked back to the office. She went into the small kitchen off the reception area, set two coffee cups on the bench, and flipped on the coffee maker. As she stood there waiting for the machine to heat, she overhead Mr G talking to someone on the phone in his office.

"My PA wouldn't have a fucking clue. The silly cow just does what she's told."

Lydia frowned. Mr G obviously hadn't realised she'd returned. She reached forward and turned off the coffee machine before it started to hiss, and inched a little closer to Mr G's door.

"So after I sorted out my management problem in Auckland, I got in touch with that guy whose number you gave me. He reckons he's free to deal me a few winning hands Saturday after next. It will be worth it to take Sam McKee down a peg. It looks bad when the help wins too much of the boss's money. If I don't stop the rot, all the other dimwits will think I'm fair game, and that would be bad for business. Besides, if I can clean Sam out, I reckon I can persuade him to do the delivery runs. Jimmy's loyal, but he's thicker than two short planks held together with stupid glue. It's only a matter of time before he fucks up and gets busted."

Lydia's forehead creased as she shook her head from side to side. She couldn't believe what she was hearing. Cheating at cards was bad enough, but planning to suck Sam into some illicit activity was despicable.

Her breath hissed softly through clenched teeth. Mr G had more money than he knew what to do with. Why did he need to cheat to get more? Even worse, why did he have to drag a good man down to his level by coercing him into something illegal?

Mr G's office went silent for a moment before he spoke again.

"Yes, maple leafs in exchange. The Mercedes will go up again early next month, so get your crews out. My buyer will take everything you can get."

Lydia tried to make sense of what she'd just heard. Were the maple leafs in his safe part of some illegal trade he had going? Moreover, what did the Mercedes have to do with it?

Confused, but more determined than ever to disentangle herself from Mr G and his company, this new information added to the long list of reasons she had to leave. Now she just needed to figure out the how and when.

Lydia padded softly over to the main entrance. Pretending to have just arrived back from buying lunch, she opened and closed the door a little more firmly this time.

"I'm back. I'll just make some coffee and bring in your lunch."

*****

Sam turned the page of his book and tried to concentrate on the words. He looked out of the window at the pelting rain, and then back to the page. The words weren't sinking in. Folding over a corner, he dropped the book onto the duvet and swung his legs off the bed.

He ran the tap and filled the kettle. The gas spluttered as he placed the kettle over the blue and yellow flame. He dropped into a chair while he waited for the water to boil.

When the intensity of the teeming rain increased even more, he stood and took three steps to the window. He placed his palms on the bench, and leaned forward, his nose near the glass. He'd never seen rain like this anywhere other than on the West Coast. The charcoal bottomed clouds looked impossibly close to the water. Sporadic lightning flashed, and thunder rumbled, reverberating off the steep hills behind him.

The rain had been pounding all morning. The thrumming on the corrugated iron roof was so loud it made sleep impossible and reading difficult. He picked up his book, and sat at the table once again.

When the kettle boiled, he looked at his watch. It had just gone noon. Grateful for something to do, he made some sandwiches to go with his cup tea.

Once he finished his lunch, he made another cuppa and drank it as he paced five steps in one direction, and then five back.

And still the rain pounded.

By 1:00 p.m. Sam had had enough and decided to go to the pub. At least at the pub, he could have a chat with Ronnie or one of the other locals he'd met during his many visits to the area. Alternately, he could watch sport on the bar's TV. With a little luck, there would be some cricket on to keep him entertained for a few hours, and stop him from going stir crazy.

He was tempted to go for a walk on the beach despite the rain, but with the amount of lightning flashing around the place, being the tallest thing on the beach was a formula for disaster. Turning himself into toast wasn't his idea of holiday fun.

Sam grabbed his wallet and car keys from the table, pulled on his oilskin, and made a dash for the Toyota.

His wipers slapped frantically on high as they tried to keep pace with the torrential rain. The rocky cliffs along the road had sprouted a number of small waterfalls as the steep land shed excess water.

As he neared the turnoff for the pub, he made a split-second decision to carry on down the Coast Road to where the man and the dog were staying, just to have a nosey, and to see if they were still in the area.

As he drove, he kept an eye out for the large shed. When it appeared through the gloom to his left, he took his foot off the accelerator and craned his neck around. The dog-owner's truck sat in the drive, water dripping off the back of its deck. Puffs of white smoke rose briefly from the cottage's chimney, only to be beaten back down by the intensity of the rain.

When he got to the Burke Road turnoff, he did a U-turn and drove past the man's house a second time on his way back to the pub. It didn't surprise him that the man was staying indoors. It was not a day to be out digging holes on the river flats.

Even the diehard coasters had given up work and gone to the pub. The car park was almost full of vehicles when Sam pulled up. The tour bus sat against the hedge on the far side, while a pair of matching campervans, an old Land Rover and various other cars and trucks were parked as close to the wooden building as possible.

He readied himself for the sprint to the veranda by re-buttoning his oilskin and securing his hat. Looking skyward, hoping for the slightest of breaks in the weather, he opened the door and splashed across the car park and up the steps.

A line of boots greeted him as he reached the entrance. Sam slipped his gumboots off, leaving them near the others, and walked into the bar in his stocking feet.

"Hi Ronnie," he said making his way past the jukebox towards the bar. "What the hell have you done with the weather?"

"Mate, if it didn't rain like this, every bastard would want to live here."

Sam chuckled at the old Coaster joke, his eye crinkling at the corners and cheeks bunching up. "Hey give me a pint of that lolly water you call lager would you. I'm feeling lucky today."

After Ronnie pulled him a pint, Sam thanked him and moved along the bar to get a better view of the TV. New Zealand was playing Australia in a one day match at the Basin Reserve in Wellington. At ninety-two for the loss of five wickets, New Zealand wasn't looking very flash, not that that surprised Sam all that much.

Despite the dismal score, being in the pub watching Australia thrash The Black Caps was better than going stir crazy in the tiny cottage. Besides, people watching on the West Coast was entertainment itself much of the time.

While Sam watched the cricket, a variety of people came in and out of the place. There wasn't much for people to do in the area if they couldn't get outside.

Even if someone didn't mind getting wet, with so much

water coming down the rivers and streams, crossing them would have been foolhardy even for experienced trampers, and working in the downpour was impossible. So, with the nearest shopping 30 odd kilometres away, and outside activities near impossible, a fair few people had found the pub a dry haven in an otherwise wet world.

An hour or after Sam arrived, a couple came into the bar with their teenage daughter. He noticed how similar the mother and daughter looked. The father's DNA hadn't figured at all.

He gave the trio a friendly nod as they passed, and watched them as they ordered burgers and chips at the end of the bar, before turning back to the cricket.

"Ahhhh ..." Sam said to nobody in particular as another Kiwi batsman's got run out trying to take a quick single. "How pathetic is that?"

The father of the girl looked back at Sam, raised his shoulders and turned his palms upward, as if to say 'what you expected something different?' before ushering his family to one of the dining tables by the fireplace.

Sam had already had two pints, so instead of another beer he ordered a large orange juice. "Oh and I'll have some spicy wedges thanks Ronnie. I need some food to soak up those beers."

Sam moved to a table by the window when the live cricket coverage stopped for the lunch break. The last thing he wanted to do was watch replays of his team crumbling to yet another outstanding bowling performance by the Australians. For a few minutes, he read the Greymouth Star, but after finishing the headlines, he put it back down again. The rain out the window continued to pour down.

This is no way to spend a holiday. I should be out finding jade.

As Sam stared numbly into the rain considering what to do for the rest of the afternoon, Ronnie placed his order in front of him.

"I see your mate's arrived."

"What?" Sam said, roused from his daydream.

"Your mate." Ronnie nodded in the direction of the car park. "You know, the one with the dog. I've been wracking my brain trying to remember where I've seen him before. It's driving me nuts."

As much as Sam wanted to whip his head around for a quick look, he managed to take a deep breath first. Leaning forward, he rested his chin on the palm of one hand, and swivelled his head in the direction of Ronnie's nod.

There he was alright. This time his dog sat in the cab next to him, ears pointed, tongue protruding. From Sam's position in the bar, it almost looked like two people were sitting in the truck.

"Hey Ronnie can I borrow your pen a tick?"

Sam jotted the man's registration number down on a coaster and slipped it into his pocket.

"I'd like to know what he's been up to on the river flats," Ronnie said, still looking out the window.

"You and me both."

The man didn't move for a moment. He sat in the truck, his chin jutting forward, eyes peering through the windscreen towards the heavens.

Sam hadn't had a close look at the man before. The closest he'd been to him was when he'd come out of the house with the gun, but even then he'd been over a hundred metres away. It had been hard to make out any features. On the beach, the man and the dog had been even further away than that.

Sam could read a lot from a person's dress and manner. After all, his father had taught him how to read people at the poker table, and he'd had plenty of practice since.

The man didn't get out at first. Sam wondered if he was waiting for a break in the rain. A moment later, the man reached across in front of the dog and grabbed what looked like a pad, and started writing something down as he looked around the car park.

"What in hell is he doing? Is he noting down registration numbers, making a shopping list or what?"

"Buggered if I know," replied Ronnie.

When the man stopped writing, he ripped the piece of paper off the pad, slipped it into his top pocket, opened the truck's door, and rushed towards the pub.

Ronnie went back to the bar.

Sam looked the other way as the man entered, but out of the corner of his eye he could see the man's face reflected in the mirror behind the bar as he ordered a beer.

The man was clean-shaven and looked to be in his early 50's. He had on a clean bush shirt, and wore high-top combat boots polished to a high gloss under camouflage pants. To Sam, the man looked like a city boy playing at being a hunter. It was the shoes that were most out of place, Coaster wore gumboots or leather work books for the most part. Combat boots, and shiny ones at that, confirmed Ronnie's theory of him being from somewhere other than the West Coast. No born and bred coaster would be seen dead wearing such shiny shoes.

After the man collected his beer, he moved further down the bar. Sam watched him surreptitiously, hoping the man wouldn't notice. Only once did he catch the man's eye. The man had turned away the moment their eyes met, but even so, in that briefest of seconds, Sam saw emotionless eyes set in a cold hard face.

Sam picked up the newspaper again to use as a shield, occasionally glancing at the man when he turned the pages.

A couple of times he caught the man looking towards the dining area. A first Sam thought he was looking at the roaring log fire Ronnie had going in the old stone fireplace, but when he studied the man's line of sight a little more closely, Sam realised he wasn't staring at the fireplace at all.

He was staring at the teenage girl.

Sam wondered if he was jumping to conclusions. Maybe the man was just checking out the assorted mining and West Coast paraphernalia Ronnie had hanging on the walls of the pub. However, when he looked again a few moments later, the man was still staring directly at the girl.

Despite the warmth in the pub, a shiver ran up Sam's spine.

He was tempted to go over and strike up a conversation, just to suss the guy out, but before he had an opportunity, the man drained the last of his beer, nodded to Ronnie, and walked out the door.

As Sam followed the man's progress towards the car park, he saw him duck briefly behind a camper van before reappearing near his truck. When the man drove off, Sam leaned towards the window so he could see which way he turned onto the main road. As suspected the truck turned north, towards the rented house.

The man's behaviour in the pub made Sam uneasy, especially the way he'd stared at the girl. Was he some sort of sicko? And, did this interest in the girl have anything to do with his odd behaviour out on the river flats?

Rather than hang around to watch the Australians bat, Sam decided to go back to the cottage for a late afternoon snooze, and to ponder this new insight about the stranger.

After saying a quick goodbye to Ronnie, Sam went out to his Toyota. As he was about to jump into the driver's side, he noticed a slip of paper tucked under a wiper blade. He grabbed hold of the paper and unfolded it. The paper was damp but the writing was still legible.

It said, 'STOP FOLLOWING ME'.

*****

After leaving the note on the Toyota, the man pulled out of the car park and turned towards his rented cottage. As he drove, he wondered if he'd made a mistake leaving the note. Maybe there was a simple reason for the Toyota stopping outside his house the previous day? Maybe the guy was having car trouble? If that were the case, his message would seem a bit strange. Alternately, if he was right, and the guy was watching them, would a few words, written on a scrap of paper, be enough to make him keep his distance?

"What do you reckon, Brutus?" The man said, turning towards his dog. "That guy seems to be turning up a little too often for my liking. Do you think he knows what we're doing?"

Brutus looked at the man and licked his lips.

As the man drove, he thought about the blond haired girl in the restaurant. His hand snaked over and gave his dog a scratch behind his ear.

"Doesn't she remind you of someone, Brutus?"

*****

"Lydia," Mr G said over the intercom, "come in here for a moment would you."

Rising from behind her desk, she opened the door of Mr G's office. "Yes?"

"I'm meeting an important client for drinks after work. We might even go to the club afterwards. I want you to go home and glam yourself up. I want to make an impression."

"What's wrong with how I'm dressed now?"

"You look fine for work, but I want you to put on something sexy, you know, show some cleavage."

Lydia clenched her jaw and put her hand on her hips. "I'm not one of your hookers you know."

"Believe me, a hooker would be a sight less hassle sometimes."

"Thanks a lot!" Lydia said, her eyes shooting daggers. "Who's the big shot anyway? He must be important if you're asking me to flash my tits. Usually you're telling me to cover up."

"Look, stop arguing and just do what you're told. I don't have the time or the inclination to explain things to you right now. Let just say that this guy helps keep you in the style to which you've become accustomed, and leave it at that. Okay?"

Lydia shrugged. "If that's the case, I'm leaving work now. I'll need a shower and time to do my makeup."

"It's just for a couple of drinks, how much time does it take to get ready for that? We'll have business to discuss afterward. You only need to stay an hour or so."

Lydia cocked her hip and just stood there scowling, not saying a word.

After thirty seconds, Mr G flicked the back of his hand in her direction. "Okay go for Christ's sake. You've got an hour and a half. We need to leave the apartment by six. Make sure you're ready on time."

Lydia turned to hide the wee smile creeping onto her face. She'd manipulated Mr G into giving her the extra time off rather than just doing what he said for a change. Having a plan to get out of Wellington was making her feel stronger and more assertive. Now she just needed to do more research on how to cover her tracks once she made her move.

Mr G heard the door slam as Lydia left the office. He picked up the phone and stood by the window, watching the traffic below as he waited for the party on the other end of the line to answer.

"Okay, it's on. I'm meeting him just after six at a wine bar in town. With luck we should make it to the club before it gets too busy. Oh and for Christ's sake, make sure Lola isn't too wasted. It's important she gets this right."

Just as the brief conversation finished, Mr G caught a glimpse of Lydia strolling down Manners Street in the direction of their apartment. He wasn't quite sure about this one. He didn't like it when she talked back. She was a lovely girl and all, but sometimes he wondered whether having a live-in girlfriend was worth the hassle. Lydia made a beautiful prop when he went out to meet business associates or city official that he needed to impress, but it wasn't as if he could tell her much about his business. She wasn't a partner in the true sense of the word. One little slip, one word to the wrong person or the IRD, and all he'd built over the last fifteen years could come crashing down.

He sat back down at his desk and reached for the bag sitting at his feet. From inside he pulled out a velvet box and set in on the desk in front of him. His share of the monthly gold run came close to forty thousand dollars, and that didn't count any of his legitimate earnings. Not bad for a man who only did one year of university before starting his first massage parlour at age twenty-two.

He lifted the lid and looked at the coins. They were a sight that always cheered him up, his retirement plan.

After putting the box back in his bag, he tidied up a few loose ends, before heading toward home. He could do with a shower and a brief rest before going out again too.

When Mr G arrived at the apartment he could hear Lydia in the bathroom.

"You still in the bath?" he said, opening the door and peering inside.

Lydia was hidden under a mountain of bubbles. "Just give me another ten minutes and it's all yours."

Mr G nodded, closed the bathroom door, and walked over to the model Mercedes. He put his bag on the floor, and reached up to turn the car, unlocking the panel hiding the safe.

After punching the combination into the keypad, a slight hiss of air sounded as the door eased opened.

Mr G grabbed the velvet box from his bag and placed it on top of the black book next to the other one. After running his finger down one edge of the stack of bundled notes, he closed the safe and went into the bedroom.

By the time Mr G was down to his boxers, Lydia was standing with towel wrapped around her, putting on her makeup.

"So how sexy do you want me?"

"I just want this guy we're meeting to be randy enough to want to go with me to the club after we have a few drinks. Okay?"

"Why the club?"

"That my darling is above your pay scale. Now get moving we've got half an hour."

Lydia felt like screaming as she walked to the bedroom. Why did he have to dangle her like a piece of meat in front of his business cronies? She took a deep breath. Keep calm, it won't be forever, she thought.

Gazing through the bedroom door towards the lounge, Lydia could see the granite plinth on the far side of the dining table. She stood there and tried to convince herself she could do it, that she could steal the money and the gold coins and disappear forever. She might even keep the black book as insurance, just in case.

By the time Mr G came out of the bathroom, Lydia had slipped on a slinky black dress with a plunging neckline. A diamond pendant nestled between the rounded curves of her breasts.

"Very nice. That should get the old boy going," Mr G said, as he looked her up and down. "I must admit you scrub up pretty good when you make an effort."

"Thanks, I think."

As Lydia put on the final touches of her makeup, Mr G put on some slacks, a silk shirt, and casual jacket. Once Lydia had made her way into the lounge, Mr G retrieved his knife from his suit jacket, and put it into his pocket. He doubted he'd need it tonight, but it had gotten to the point where he felt naked without it.

"You ready?" Mr G called out.

"Just give me a minute. I want to take an aspirin. I feel a headache coming on."

"Better yet, don't take it. It will look more convincing when you make your excuse to leave."

Chapter 11 - Friday Evening

Steam rose from the cup of tea in Sam's hand as he sat pondering the note on the table in front of him. Finding the piece of paper under his wiper blade had given him a shock. He hadn't realised the man even knew of his existence, let alone knew he had taken a passing interest in his activities. This note put a whole new perspective on things.

Why did the man feel the need to warn him off? What secret did he have that made his presence such a worry? Was the guy even rational?

The more he thought about the note, the more puzzled he became. Had the man seen him follow his trail to the shallow hole up on the flats somehow? Worse, was there some way he'd been sprung checking out the rented house? Sam hadn't seen any sight of him until he had walked out of the house with the shotgun. Had the man seen him through a window? Both options seemed unlikely.

While mulling over the possibilities, Sam leaned forward and rubbed his temples with his thumb and forefinger. A few minutes later, he got up and rummaged though his stuff looking for some aspirin.

After swallowing a couple of tablets with the last of his tea, he pulled out his cell phone and powered it up. He danced around the cottage holding the phone up high and down low trying to get a signal. After a few minutes he gave up and threw on his oilskin. He'd have to drive towards Greymouth until he got within range of a cell phone tower.

The drive from the cottage south towards Greymouth was spectacular. He had a number of bluffs and switchbacks to negotiate, all of which streamed with impromptu waterfalls cascading from the cliffs and rushing down the gullies, making it quite an exciting expedition. In places, small rocks, and slips, complete with clumps of fern and moss, had tumbled onto the main road. Sam was surprised how fast the steep landscape shed the torrential rain it had been getting over the last twelve hours. There wasn't another district in the country that could have coped with such a deluge without there being major flooding.

Just past Rapahoe, along the Seven Mile Road a few kilometres north of Runanga, he finally got a couple of bars on his phone and pulled onto the shoulder.

"Tane Jackson," the voice on the other end of the phone said.

"Hi Tane, Sam McKee."

"Sammy boy, long time. What can I do for you?"

"Hey sorry to bother you mate, but I need you to run a plate for me."

"No problem brother. Hang on, I'll just grab a pen."

While Sam waited, he pulled the bar coaster with the truck's registration number on it out of his pocket.

"So how fast do you need this?" Tane asked, after jotting the rego number down. "Monday okay?"

"That will be great. I'm out of cell range a lot at the moment so just leave a message if I don't pick up. I don't suppose you could have a quick look to see if the owner has a record while you're at it? I'm working a job and it sure would be a big help."

"I can't guarantee anything, but I'll see what I can do."

"That's all I can ask," Sam said. "Oh and say hello to that lovely wife of yours."

"I will, you have a good weekend. Stay out of trouble."

"You too amigo."

Sam closed his phone and put it back in his pocket. He didn't know what he'd do with the information once he had it, but he did know that having too much information was always better than not having enough. In his business, information was king.

As he drove back towards the cottage, he noticed the clouds were lifting. Small patches of blue were beginning to poke through the grey in the distance. Rain still fell, but it had eased in intensity.

With a little luck he might have a chance to go jade hunting in the morning. Nothing he knew cleared his head and sorted his thoughts faster than a long walk down the beach.

*****

Dodging and weaving, Mr G guided Lydia towards the bar. The Friday night crowd was close packed and rocking good-naturedly to the music. Mr G slapped a $100 note on the mahogany bar.

"A bottle of Marlborough Pinot Gris and three glasses thanks." he said, before pointing towards a secluded table near the back. "Is that our table? The name's Graeme."

"Yes sir. If you'd like to take your seat, I'll bring your wine right over."

As the waiter poured the wine, Mr G noticed a slightly overweight man wearing an ill-fitting suit come into the bar. Mr G stood, caught his attention, and then turned to Lydia. "Remember sweetheart, a little flirting is good for business."

Lydia looked at the man on his way to their table and downed half her glass in one gulp. "You said an hour right?"

"Just play nice."

Mr G held his hand out as the man neared, "Len, sit. I'm so pleased you could make it. This is my PA Lydia."

Len shook Mr G's hand, "Thanks for the invite Mr Graeme. I haven't been here before. It's a bit out of my price range." Then he turned briefly towards Lydia doing his best to look her in the eye without letting his gaze drop to her chest.

Mr G pulled out a chair and waved Len into it.

"Don't you worry about that Len, it's my shout. After all, you're doing me a favour here. Your expertise will help me enormously. But let's not talk about that now. We're here to have some fun."

"Can I pour you a wine Len?" Lydia asked. "You've got some catching up to do."

Lydia did her best to pay Len some attention, but her headache showed in her eyes.

"You still have that headache?" Mr G asked her after forty-five minutes.

"I'm sorry," Lydia said. "And I was so looking forward to tonight."

"Hey it's not your fault. You go on home, I'm sure Len and I will manage without you."   Mr G turned to Len. "Hey, what say I ring a cab? We can drop Lydia home on the way to dinner. There's a great little Thai place across the road from my club."

Len wasn't too fussed what he did. Mr G had kept his glass topped up so it had been hard for him to keep track of how much he'd been drinking. After the first couple of glasses, he'd found it harder and harder to keep his eyes off Lydia, especially when she leaned forward to pick up her wine glass and her flimsy top gaped open.

Len blinked a couple of times and shook his head. "Okay Mr Graham, food's probably a good idea. I don't normally drink this much."

Once they'd dropped Lydia back at the apartment, the cab doubled back towards the Thai restaurant.

"Ah Mr G, welcome back," a young Thai woman said as they entered. "Come I have a nice table for you by the window."

"Have you eaten here before Len? The Tom Yum Goong and Pad Thai are superb."

Len's eyes were blank. "Um …"

"Why don't I order for both of us and we can share, that way you'll get a taste of everything?

With the food, Mr G ordered another bottle of wine. The waitress filled two glasses when it arrived.

"Cheers," Mr G said lifting his glass, "and thanks again for coming out tonight."

A *ting* rang out across their table as their glasses touched.

"Lydia's quite a honey isn't she Len? I think she liked you." Mr G said, knowing full well Len was married and had two school-aged children.

The two men talked a little about planning consents and permits for a new development Mr G had in the wings, but Mr G kept bringing the conversation back to the two new girls who had just started work at his club across the road.

"You should see them Len. Sarah's got these firm breasts

and legs that go on forever but Lola … Wow, she has got to be the hottest girl I've ever had working for me."

"Do you, um. Do you ever … you know?"

Mr G gave Len a wink. "Of course. Not much point being the boss if I didn't test the merchandise now and then is there?"

Len's lewd grin told Mr G all he needed to know.

"Why don't we pop over for a while after dinner? We can catch the show from my VIP booth and have a coffee to sober you up before you go home to your wife."

Forty minutes later, they sat in a padded booth next to the runway style stage, opposite one of the two poles that graced its length. On the pole in front of them, a young woman wearing nothing but a G-string spun and twisted, holding herself aloft using only her muscular legs. Further down the runway, another woman with dark hair and olive skin danced suggestively in front of a man holding a handful of bills in his hand. Every time she neared the man, she extended her thigh so he could tuck another note into her garter.

"Lola's on next," Mr G said turning to Len. "Wait till you get an eyeful of her."

Len's eyes were already like saucers as he ogled the girl dancing in front of him. Mr G couldn't wait to see his reaction when Lola came out.

A microphone crackled.

"Thank you ladies and gentlemen, let's give a big hand to Sarah and Miffy," the MC said. "Now for your entertainment, let's welcome our newest dancer all the way from Sydney, Australia. Give it up for the stunning, the beautiful, the incredibly sexy, Lola Devine!"

The music started as the lights dimmed to a single spot. From behind a red curtain glided a tall slim blond with hair halfway down the middle of her back. The white leather vest she wore pushed her breasts together and up to the point where they seemed ready to tumble out at any moment.

As Lola danced, tassels on the front of her vest rotated in hypnotic fashion, drawing the viewer's eyes to her biggest assets. Slung low on her hips were the shortest of shorts accentuating her long legs and bronzed skin.

Lola slowly danced and gyrated her way down the stage towards the two men sitting in the VIP booth, finally coming to a stop opposite Len.

Mr G turned to gauge Len's reaction to Lola's dance, and smiled when he saw the slack-jawed, near drooling expression plastered across his face.

With her legs wide apart and thrusting her backside out behind her, Lola bent forward at the waist, twirling her tassels and motioning Len to undo the small clasp holding the vest together in the front.

"Go on Len, she wants you to unhook her," Mr G said, nodding in the girls direction. "Go for it man. Release those puppies."

Len stood and reached toward the girls vest, a tremor visible in his hands. After a little fiddling, he finally managed to undo the clasps and Lola moved her hands up to cover herself as the vest dropped onto the stage.

Before Len had a chance to sit, Lola grabbed his wrists, and pulled him forward, placing his hands on her breasts. Len licked his lips as he squeezed gently looking directly into Lola's sparkling blue eyes. Then with a playful laugh and a flick of her hair, she turned back to the pole and started the rest of her routine.

"I think she likes you Len," Mr G said. "I've never seen her do that with a customer before."

Len sat stunned, eyes riveted on where, only moments before, his hands had been.

Five minutes later, the MC was back on the microphone. "Gentlemen, let's give it up for the beautiful, the amazing, the unbelievable, Lola Divine!"

"Come on Len, let's go meet a few of the girls. I've got an office backstage where we can have a little privacy."

Mr G stood without waiting for Len's answer, and led him through a side door to the left of the MC's booth and down a short hallway to a comfortable room with two wide leather couches and, unbeknownst to Len, a two-way mirror.

"Grab a seat Len, make yourself comfortable."

A few minutes later, Lola came into the office carrying a bottle of champagne and wearing nothing but a smile and a rhinestone G-string.

"Hi there handsome, a little birdie told me you'd be in here."

Poor old Len didn't stand a chance.

*****

When Lydia got back to the apartment she took a couple of aspirin, put on some sweat pants and a t-shirt, and lay down on the bed with her laptop. If history was anything to go by, Mr G would be hours. She'd gotten used to him turning up drunk and smelling of other women.

The very first time she'd accused him of fooling around, he swore it was all part of being a club owner, of being a good host.

"What are the punters meant to think if I'm afraid to put my arm around the girls," Mr G had said one time after she'd complained of him smelling of cheap perfume. "That's not very good advertising is it?"

Lydia didn't care anymore. If Mr G was out shagging one of his girls, he wasn't demanding sex at home, and that suited her just fine.

Once Lydia's lap top booted up, she typed 'Paris apartments' into Google.

The first entry showed short-stay apartments close to the centre of town from as little as twenty-nine pounds a night with a twenty percent discount for more than three nights.

Further down the page, she saw the one she wanted. It had views of the Seine from the top floor of a charming nineteenth century stone building. The interior walls were pure white, with a large canopy bed dressed beautifully in white linen. A white tiled kitchen, with new appliances, was just off the main room. A marble bathroom, complete with claw-foot bath and separate shower, ran off a small alcove that contained a washing machine and tumble dryer.

The Trocadero Gardens and the Eiffel Tower were within easy walking distance, and restaurants and cafes abounded in the area. All this for only 800 Euros a week.

This was exactly the style of place Lydia dreamed of staying in. During the day she'd stroll along the banks of the Seine, a book on Napoleon, or some famous artist under her arm. She'd sit in the cool shade of a centuries-old stone bridge as ferries, barges, and other craft plied the blue-grey waters. Maybe a handsome man like Sam McKee would approach and ask her if she'd like to accompany him to a nearby cafe for a kir or pastis. What could be better?

Lydia gave her head a shake.

"Wake up", she told herself. "You've got to figure out how to get over there without that arsehole knowing where you've gone first."

She wondered what search terms she should try to find out that sort of information? She typed 'escape without a trace' into Google and hit the enter button.

Seconds later, a list of websites claiming to be able to help people disappear came up on the screen before her.

Her eyes scanned back and forth.

Misinformation, it seemed, was a high priority. One website stressed the need to leave believable clues that would lead her followers down a false trail and gain her valuable time.

Most importantly, she'd need a false passport and other papers to create a new identity. But where in the hell would she obtain those? Lydia felt a little tremor of fear run through her. Creating an escape plan was starting to look a lot more difficult that she'd first thought. So many things she'd have to take into account, things she'd need to figure out without Mr G catching on. One little slip and she'd be out on the street looking for a new job and a new place to live at best. At worst, God only knew what Mr G was capable of.

Lydia logged off and leaned back on her pillows, staring at the ceiling. She thought once again about the contents of the safe, remembering what she'd seen when she opened the black book, the names of prominent people with dollar amounts next to them.

Maybe she was looking at this whole thing from the wrong angle. Maybe someone needed to inform the police of Mr G's criminal activities and the existence of the black book in his possession. How many years in jail would a person get for bribery and blackmail?

Not enough most likely, Mr G could afford the best lawyers. Would police even have grounds for a search warrant on the basis of one anonymous phone call? It was unlikely. Optimistically, assuming she could interest police in his criminal activities, Mr G might get a year or two. But would that be enough time for her to sort out a bogus passport, develop a new identity, and disappear for good?

Maybe she could change her name by deed poll. Her grandfather had been English. If she could get a British passport, she could enter any EU countries without the need for a visa. That might work.

Lydia caught herself drifting off as she dreamed of travel. She turned off her computer, pulled back the duvet and snuggled into its softness. A quick look at her watch as she placed it on the bedside table showed it had just gone midnight. It was time to get to some sleep. Mr G could be home any time, better if she wasn't awake when that happened.

She wondered how Len was getting on. She could just imagine how out of place he'd be in a strip club. Mr G's girls would eat the poor man alive, although somehow, she figured, that's exactly what Mr G had in mind. She'd have to remember to have a look through the company records on Monday morning when she went to work, and figure out what project Mr G was grooming him to fast track.

Lydia wasn't sure what time it was when the front door of the apartment clunked shut. After hearing the water in the kitchen tap run, and footsteps enter the bedroom Lydia cracked open one eye ever so slightly and caught sight of Mr G wobbling his way to the ensuite. After flushing the toilet, he bumped into the mattress as he made his way to his side of the bed.

"Bugger," Mr G mumbled as he tripped on his trouser legs while undressing. He reached out to steady himself and banged the wall. "Shuuuussssh ..."

From all the noise, Lydia could tell he was really drunk. In addition, he reeked. She could smell the brandy on him before he even got into bed. She closed her eyes and lay absolutely still. The last thing she needed was an inebriated Mr G getting frisky. The slob hadn't even bothered to brush his teeth.

Chapter 12 - Saturday Morning

Sun streamed through patches of blue sky as Sam looked out the cottage window towards the hills to the east. The mist had gone and the air was crystal clear. Each tree and bush looked sharp and in focus. Flowering rata trees dotted the canopy with patches of red, and he could see a pair of New Zealand Falcons soaring the thermals along the high cliffs searching for prey.

He made himself breakfast and ate while reading the paper. According to the chart, the tide was just turning so there was no great hurry to rush off.

He planned to head back to Burke Road today, but rather than walking north towards the midden, he wanted to check the beach to the south towards Barrytown for a change. There were a couple of spots he wanted to check, places he'd found jade on previous trips.

After heating a large pot of water on the gas burner, he had a quick sponge bath, not bothering to light the fire to heat water for a shower, brushed his teeth and packed up his gear.

As he drove pass the village, he saw Ronnie outside sweeping the veranda, his red hair glowing like a beacon in the crisp morning light. Sam tooted his horn. Ronnie looked up from his work and waved.

When Sam passed the large shed, he slowed to 50 kph and craned his neck around for a good look at the rented house. The white truck wasn't in the driveway, but faint wisps of smoke were still rising from the chimney. Sam suspected the man and dog hadn't been gone long. Would they already be in the car park at Burke Road when he got there?

With only one way to find out, Sam turned onto the gravel and made his way the kilometre down to the beach. Steam rose off the quickly drying road as he dodged puddles and a lone weka feeding near the verge.

When he reached the car park, it was empty. He'd have the beach to himself after all. Without wasting any time, he grabbed his gear and locked the Toyota. Skirting the left hand edge of the creek, he wove his way down to the high tide mark.

Waves pounded the beach, pushed ashore from a storm further out in the Tasman Sea. From what Sam could tell from the patterns in the sand, the last tide had been a high one. There was a distinct line marking where the waves had crept up the shingle bank during the night. With luck, that action would have exposed some new jade as well.

It looked a perfect day for beachcombing.

He assumed his standard hunting pace, eyes swinging right, then left, and back again, along the line of driftwood and newly tumbled stones. He tried not to focus too hard as he scanned the pebbles on the beach. His goal was to 'get in the zone' as he liked to call it — a Zen-like state where he could see everything, yet nothing — where a glint of green would trigger a subconscious recognition, turning his brain into a highly efficient jade detector.

The angled sunlight on the still damp stones made them shine. Jade, theoretically, should glisten considerably more than the greywacke and quartz around it making it more obvious to the hunter. Sam's gut told him it was a good day for finding treasure.

Every now and then Sam looked up, taking notice of the scene around him — the gentle curve of the beach, the clouds, the way the light reflected off the ocean. This act reminded him of his dad and the times they used to go walking. He could almost hear his father's words in his head.

"You'll miss all the wonder if you don't remember to look up Sammy," his dad had said all those years ago. "Far better to trip and fall occasionally than spend your whole life looking at the dirt."

His father had been right. This place was a wonder. The stunning landscape that greeted him, made him feel like the only person on the planet. With little effort, he could imagine how the first explorers must have felt coming along this beach hundreds of years ago. How rugged and foreboding the area would have seemed with its impossibly steep mountains rising from the sea to the east, huge towering peaks far off to the south, and the sea pounding relentlessly towards land from the west. Without the benefit of roads or tracks, it would have taken early visitors to the West Coast months just to get here.

After doing a 360-degree rotation and scanning to the horizon in every direction, Sam's eyes dropped back to the beach as he resumed his search.

A few minute later, a flash of green caught his eye. He bent down to pick up a small pebble and rubbed it on his trousers. When it dried grey, he dropped it and kept walking. Five minutes later, he came to a patch of beach where there were pieces of chalk-white quartz, rounded over time, each about the size and shape of a slightly flattened orange. He grabbed half a dozen and slipped them into his daypack.

These pieces of quartz he'd give to friends as a souvenir of the West Coast. His friends found the quartz an odd present at first, but when Sam told them that, when rubbed together, these stones would create light, or triboluminescence as the scientists called it, the gifts made more sense.

"This quartz reminds me of how you two light up when you are close to each other," Sam had told some good friends on their engagement. "Keep them as a reminder that you need to rub together often if you're going to keep that spark going."

The quartz also reminded Sam of his last relationship. How that spark had gradually died. Not that it was anyone's fault. They'd both tried to make it work, but for whatever reason the passion that had kick-started their getting together, wasn't sustainable. Unfortunately, they didn't have enough in common for that not to matter. In the end, they'd both decided it was best just to walk away.

That had been two years ago, and although a few friends had set him up with dates, he'd never gone out with any of them for more than a week or two. Only one had ever made it into his bedroom.

When Sam reached the first major creek, he could see it was going to be tricky to cross. Despite the rain having stopped, a huge amount of water still had to make its way to the sea.

The action of the creek had cut away the sand, creating a

deep channel that looked mid-thigh deep with water moving at a speed fast enough to wash someone off their feet. If the surf had been less violent, he would have walked closer to sea's edge, where the creek fanned out across the beach a little more as it merged with the waves. But that was impossible with the tide still having a fair way to go out and a big beach-break crashing onto the shore.

Rather than risk crossing, Sam made his way further inland to see if there was a safer option upstream, some stepping stones, or a fallen tree perhaps.

He crested the shingle bank and followed the edge of the creek inland for a couple of hundred metres, until he came to a section where the creek broadened out and looked only shin-deep. The water was still racing along, but being shallower, Sam felt confident he could ford the stream without putting himself at risk.

He was looking for a stout branch to use for support, when a fountain of sand kicked up at his feet.

Sam was confused by the eruption, but only for a second.

The next shot hit rock. CRACK!

Sam threw himself on the ground and swivelled his head around. "What the fuck ..."

After twenty seconds or so, he raised up to a crouch and began working his way back towards the beach, keeping as low as possible as he went. He certainly didn't want to stay put. He might become a sitting target if he did that.

Once he crested the shingle bank, he ducked behind a flax bush growing on its rim and looked back. He saw movement on the other side of the creek near the edge of a grove of beech trees, but was too far away to tell if it was a person hiding, or just the breeze moving the branches around.

In either case, Sam didn't feel like hanging around.

He scurried down the bank to the beach and started jogging, trying to put as much distance between himself and the shooter as possible. Every twenty metres or so, he snuck a glance over his shoulder, planning to zigzag up the bank and into the bushes, at the first sight of someone pointing anything vaguely looking like a gun in his direction.

Sam was thankful that the creek was up. At least the shooter wouldn't be able to follow without first working their way across the torrent. By then he planned to be far away.

The further he got from the creek, the less his nerves rattled. His shoulders began to relax and he looked back less often. Gradually, his pace slowed to a brisk walk, and he started replaying the event in his mind.

He considered the terrain around the creek, and realised that the shot had to have come from the far side. The land on the Burke Road side of the creek had been cleared for dairy farming. It was relatively flat and there was nowhere for a shooter to hide. Whereas on the Barrytown side, much of the land, due to its boggy nature, had flax bushes, small stands of tree ferns and Southland beech to hide in.

Sam pictured the topography of the area in his mind, as if looking down at it on a map. From the end of Burke Road he'd walked about half an hour. But his pace hadn't been very quick, and he'd paused often to pick up things along the way. He figured he'd made maybe three kilometres at most. The beach ran almost parallel to the Coast road, apart from where it jutted in and out around a couple of minor headlands.

Who would have cause to be in the area just over the creek? There'd been no other cars in the car park, and there was no way someone could have passed him without his knowledge. Whoever had fired at him must have either come north from Barrytown, where there was a small parking area at the beach end of the village's main street, cut across one of the farmer's paddocks from the highway, or come down the creek by the …

Then Sam remembered that the dog owner's rented cottage was nestled in the bush 100 metres or so across the scrubby ground on the far side of the creek.

The more Sam considered the idea the more sense it made. He knew the man had a gun. The location made sense seeing the man's rented accommodation was the only house in the vicinity. Then there was the note. It all added up.

After getting back to his Toyota in record time, Sam took out his phone and looked at its face, knowing the chances of having a signal were slim. When he saw the out of service notification, he decided to go to the pub and call the cops from there.

Then he stopped and considered the situation a moment. It would take a police car at least half an hour to drive up from Greymouth. By the time he gave them a statement, and they drove to where the incident had taken place, well over an hour would have passed and any chance of finding the shooter would be gone.

Even if he told police of his suspicions regarding the man with the dog, without any evidence, what could he expect the police to do? Besides, if the man was paranoid, the police turning up at his door might intensify the man's delusions. The last thing Sam wanted to do was push some nut-bar over the edge.

Whether he decided to call the cops or not, he'd worked up a thirst during his quick retreat from the beach.

There was still no sign of the man's truck when Sam drove past, which seemed odd. But then maybe the man had driven off after the incident, worried he might get a visit from the cops.

Sam pondered the situation as he cruised down the Coast Road. When he got to the village, he turned into Cargill's Road and pulled up outside the pub.

Just as Sam got out of his Toyota, Ronnie drove into the car park and started unloading a jute sack full of white stones onto one of the pub's many rockeries.

"Are you trying to rid the beach of quartz there Ronnie?"

"Take more than me to do that. That last tide sure churned things up."

"You didn't happen to see that guy with the dog on the beach today did you?"

"Nah, I was just down this end collecting for the garden. I saw a few people further down the beach, but no dog. Why?"

"I've just been up near that big creek south of Burke Road, and some prick took a couple of pot shots at me."

"Jesus you sure?"

"Fucking oath I'm sure. You should have heard the ricochet."

"You want to use the phone to call the cops?" Ronnie asked as the two of them climbed the steps and entered the bar.

"Not a lot of point is there? Whoever it was will be long gone by now."

"We often get dickheads from Christchurch coming over here to blast a few rounds off over the weekend. How close were they … the shots I mean? Maybe some idiot was shooting rabbits and didn't see you."

"They were too bloody close for comfort, believe me. By the time I stopped eating dirt and had a chance to look around, I couldn't see anyone. I suspect they were in that patch of scrub between the road and that rental house just north of Burke Road."

"The old Johansen Place? Yeah I know it. That where the dog guy is staying?"

"I believe so. His truck was parked there when I drove past yesterday. He's not there today though."

"Hmmm …" Ronnie said, scratching at the stubble on his face. "But you still think it might have been him?"

"The thought had crossed my mind."

Ronnie wandered around behind the bar and started wiping down the countertop. "But how would you prove it, eh?"

"Exactly," Sam said. "Anyway, after jogging back to the car park I'm drier than Central Otago in the summertime. Give me a pint of that gnat's piss you Coasters seem to be so fond of."

"No problem. Would you like some lemonade in that city boy?" Ronnie asked with a smirk. "I'd hate for you to get so drunk you piss yourself."

*****

Lydia had been up for almost two hours by the time Mr G finally surfaced. His bloodshot eyes were a testament to the late night and the amount of alcohol he'd consumed.

"You look like you could do with a coffee," she said.

Mr G wobbled into the kitchen still dressed in his robe. "Jesus, my fucking head," he said before slumping down on a chair at the table. "Seems Len's a bigger drinker than I gave him credit for."

"So, is he going to help you out now that you've bought him dinner and let him shag one of your sluts?"

"Don't you bleeding well start. You're quite happy to live here aren't you? Do you think the money to keep this place going just floats down from the sky you silly moo? I work hard and it's not always easy, so give me a bloody break."

Lydia put a cup of coffee in front of Mr G and turned back to her cleaning, wishing she hadn't hassled him, especially when he was hung-over. She had nothing to gain by irritating him, best just to play happy families ... for the time being anyway.

Mr G had just poured himself a second cup of coffee when the phone rang. "What?" he growled into the receiver.

"That you Mr G?" Jimmy said.

"Who the fuck else would it be? You think maybe the prime bloody minister is going to answer my phone on a Saturday morning?"

Lydia raised her eyebrows as she listened to the conversation. Mr G could be such a prick sometimes.

"Sorry Mr G, it's just that we got a problem."

Mr G exhaled sharply and put the palm of his hand over his eyes. "What sort of problem?"

"It's Ethan, he's done a runner."

"That ungrateful little ..."

"I swung by his place to check up on him like you asked, but his landlady told me he'd packed his bags and moved out yesterday morning. All his stuff is gone."

"Fuck, now I'll have to come up and organise a replacement."

"I could run the place for you Mr G."

Jimmy running his brothel would be like putting an alcoholic in charge of a brewery. "Thanks Jimmy but you're too important where you are in my organisation. Who else could I trust to drive the Mercedes?"

"Yeah I suppose."

"I'll catch the 9:00 a.m. flight up tomorrow morning. Be there to pick me up. Okay?"

Lydia smiled when she heard the last part of Mr G's conversation. It sounded like she was going to have some more time to herself soon. More time to plan.

"You hear that?" Mr G asked her as she passed.

"About the flight to Auckland you mean?"

"Yeah, jump online and book me a flight while I have a shower would you? Then cook me something to eat. I'm starving."

Lydia sang softly under her breath as she made Mr G a ham and cheese croissant and a leafy green salad. She was pleased to have some more free time to look forward to. After Mr G left in the morning, she'd check out some travel websites, and do some more investigation into what it would take for her to get a British Passport. She'd also have a closer look at the papers in Mr G's safe.

As she tossed the salad, she wondered how many of the papers would incriminate Mr G. If she kept copies, and threatened to give them to the authorities, would that be enough to protect her from his anger once he realised the money was missing?

She had just set Mr G's meal on the table when he came out of the bedroom.

"You get that ticket booked?"

"Yes you're on the 9:05. Now sit down and eat. I've made croissants."

Mr G looked down at the plate half filled with salad and frowned. "Fucking croissants, and salad? Do I look like some French fucking rabbit? I said COOK me some lunch you daft cow. Ever heard of bacon and fucking eggs?"

"But I thought ..."

"That's the problem, you don't fucking think. I've had enough of you and all this French shit. Ever since we got back from Paris all you can talk about it how the bloody Frogs do things. If I have to eat one more fucking croissant I'll go fucking bonkers."

"Why didn't you say something?"

"How many times do I have to suggest you cook steak or lamb before you get the hint? Why do you think I keep taking you out to eat? Fuck it. I've had enough of you anyway. Look, I'm going to be in Auckland for a couple days. When I get back I want you gone. Do you hear me? Just fuck off! I'm going to pack a bag. I'll be at the club until my flight."

And with that Mr G stormed off.

"What? You—you want me to go?" Lydia said not quite believing what she'd just heard.

Mr G stuck his head back through the bedroom door. "Yes, and while I'm at it, you're fired. Give me your keys to the office. I'll transfer three months pay into your account from Auckland. There are some serviced apartment on The Terrace, take your crap and book yourself into one. Believe me, you don't want to be here when I get back."

Lydia felt her knees wobble. She took two unsteady steps and sat down onto a chair, shaking her head and wondering how she hadn't seen it coming. BANG, just like that, kicked out.

In one way she felt like laughing. Mr G had just supplied her with an exit. Here she was thinking he'd be heartbroken, that he'd stalk her if she tried to leave. Instead, he'd biffed her out without a care. She wondered if his bitterness had been building up for a while and she just hadn't noticed, or if Mr G was unhinged, and all it had taken was an A-grade hangover to make him snap.

In either case, this new development changed things. Now, rather than being able to plan an orderly disappearance, she either had to find somewhere to live and get another job, or she had to take the money and run.

Lydia tried to tell herself this new development was a blessing in disguise, but as her eyes misted up, she wasn't so sure. Being dumped, even by someone she planned to leave, still hurt, especially when it was so sudden and done in such a callous manner.

A few minutes later, Mr G came out of the bedroom carrying a small suitcase. "Where's your key to the office?"

Lydia went to the silver tray and took the key off her key ring and handed it over. "You said three months pay didn't you?"

"Yes, and you can keep the jewellery. It's all paste anyway. Just clean up after yourself before you go and leave the key to the apartment on the bench on your way out. I could say it's been fun, but I'd be lying. What the fuck I was thinking when I moved you in, I'll never know."

Lydia winced as the door slammed.

A sob escaped her lips as she rested her face in the palms of her hands. Tears dripped from between her fingers onto the floor. Rejection was a new experience for her. She hadn't realised until now how much it hurt.

Lydia felt sorry for herself until she remembered the safe full of money. Then she got angry. "Stop being a sook!"

She gritted her teeth, rose from the table, and dried her eyes with a tissue. She tried to cheer herself up by picturing the stacks of $100 notes and the gold Mapleleafs in her mind, and by remembering the Paris apartment she'd seen online. Before long, her face began to relax and the corners of her mouth twitched up. The next thing she knew, she was beaming, bright as a full moon rising.

Chapter 13 - Sunday Morning

After his near miss the day before, Sam decided to stay well away from Burke Road. If the man with the dog had taken a couple of shots at him, he was obviously unhinged. Sam saw no point in provoking him further. Instead, he planned to drive south past Greymouth and on to Serpentine Creek, where jade and premium pieces of chatoyant serpentine could be found.

He needed to restock his supplies in any case. His plan was to spend a few hours beachcombing. Afterwards, he'd stop at the supermarket on his way back to the cottage. As a treat, he might even pick up some whitebait for dinner.

As he passed through Runanga on his way south, his cell phone beeped. He pulled over to the shoulder of the road. It was a text message from Mr G inviting him to a poker game the Saturday after next. Mr G had a friend coming down from Auckland who was keen for a game. It seemed Mr G didn't want to disappoint him.

The timing might work out just about right. Another week or so and Sam would be ready for a few city comforts, especially if it involved taking more cash off Mr G and his cronies. Another game like the last one and he might be able to afford a luxury trip to the Coromandel Peninsula to do some gold panning. Who knows, he might even upgrade his trusty old Toyota.

Sam chuckled as he pulled back out onto the highway.

You're a glutton for punishment Mr G.

*****

Out of the bedroom window, Lydia saw a jet climbing northwards over the harbour. She picked up her watch from the bedside cabinet. It read 9:02 a.m. Mr G's flight to Auckland was right on time.

She threw back the duvet and stepped into the ensuite. The shower hissed as she swung the mixer around into the red. As the water steamed, she dropped her knickers and the old t-shirt she'd slept in onto the floor and examined herself in the mirror. She tested the weight of each breast in the palms of her hands, before turning sideways and patting her flat stomach.

"This is wasted on him," she said to her reflection. "Mr G can have his strippers for all I care."

She opened the shower door, tested the water with her hand, and climbed in. Jets of warm water beat a solid stream onto her back as she twisted and stretched her muscles awake. As she showered, she made a mental list of the things she needed to do.

Mr G had really thrown her plans out of wack by kicking her out of the apartment. He would only be gone for a couple of days. How could she possibly arrange everything she needed to do in such a short length of time?

Could she even smuggle that much gold out of the country? She doubted it. The airport's metal detectors would be buzzing and flashing before she got anywhere near a plane, not to mention the trouble she'd be in if customs found that much cash on her. How would she explain that?

If she travelled overseas in the next day or so, she'd have to use her New Zealand passport, making it easy for someone to trace her. She couldn't see a lot of point in going somewhere where she didn't know her way around and couldn't speak the language, just to have Mr G or one of his associates find her in the first week.

Besides, she'd be vulnerable in a place she didn't know, tourists went missing all the time overseas. Who would miss one more?

"God what a mess," she mumbled as she got out of the shower and reached for a towel. Was it even worth the risk?

Maybe taking the three months severance pay and slinking away with her tail between her legs was a more sensible option. Did she want to be looking over her shoulder for the rest of her life?

As she dried herself off, Lydia thought about Sam, wondering where he might be.

She made a mental note to warn him about the poker game. She loved the idea of Sam taking some more money off the grumpy old bastard. It would serve him right for being a cheat.

After she dressed and made herself a cup of coffee, she retrieved the combination from her handbag and went over to the safe. She opened the front panel and punched in the numbers.

As the loot came into view, Lydia whistled. Even seeing it a second time gave her the tingles. When she leaned forward, she noticed the second box of coins and wondered when Mr G had put them there.

"You crafty bugger."

Placing the two boxes on the floor, Lydia carried the three ring binders and the black diary to the table and started reading through them, trying to work out if there was enough incriminating evidence contained within to put serious pressure on Mr G, should she choose to carry on and steal the money. Unless she could figure a way to insure against Mr G's wrath, all the money on the planet wouldn't help her.

As she suspected, the ring binders contained business stuff, mainly contracts, leases and the like. None of them, from what she could tell, contained illegal or incriminating material.

The diary was another story altogether. There was page after page of contact details, notes on specific transactions, bribes and dates, organised to perfection. Tucked in the back of the book was a CD-rom.

Lydia took the CD over to the table, grabbed her laptop from its bag and booted it up.

"This should be interesting." She slipped the disk into the player. A dialogue box popped up asking her if she wanted to open the folder. After clicking yes, a series of thumbnails, popped up on screen. Most of the pictures were of different men taken in compromising positions with young women in various stages of undress, cavorting on a wide leather sofa.

Lydia caught her breath when she recognised a couple of people she'd seen in the newspaper or on TV. No wonder Mr G had been so successful in business. She could imagine the power possessing these pictures would give him over those whose job it was to protect the public against men just like him.

The only problem Lydia could see was how to link this material to Mr G. Not once had she seen his name mentioned, nor was he in any of the photographs. From an evidential perspective, this book could have come from anywhere. Did she really want to involve the cops if there wasn't absolute proof of Mr G's involvement? Maybe the threat of police would be enough. Or maybe if the people Mr G was blackmailing discovered he no longer had control of the incriminating evidence, they would come down on him like a pack of angry animals freed from their cages, and do a better job destroying Mr G than the police could ever do. Now wouldn't that teach him a lesson?

*****

Sam put the last bag of groceries in the back seat of the Toyota and drove off looking for somewhere to buy fresh whitebait. He drove along the banks of the Grey River where he'd seen stalls selling the delicacy on previous trips.

Half a kilometre along, opposite a weatherboard pub built in the late 1800s, he saw a guy sitting under a beach umbrella with a chilly bin. Forty dollars later he came back to the Toyota clutching a frozen packet wrapped in newspaper.

"Fritters for dinner, yum," he said, imagining the delicate flavours that would soon be bursting in his mouth.

As he neared the cottage, he decided to drive the extra couple of kilometres to the pub for a beer before cooking up his feast. His curiosity about the man and his dog nagged at him like a festering mosquito bite.

Would the man dare show his face at the pub again after taking pot shots at him?

That's assuming it was him, Sam reminded himself.

Maybe Ronnie was right. Maybe the shots had come from some moronic hunter who'd failed to identifying his background properly before pulling the trigger. It wouldn't be the first time. Every year people got killed by hunters who'd made the same stupid mistake. He hadn't actually seen the shooter had he? Maybe they hadn't seen him either? Was he jumping to conclusions because of where the incident took place?

Sam considered the issue all the way to Barrytown. When he saw the village coming up, he turned off the main road and pulled up outside the pub.

There was no sign of the white truck. Sam didn't know whether to be relieved or disappointed. Conflict with the dog owner was the last thing he wanted, but he wouldn't let the man run him off the beach either.

After pulling on the handbrake, Sam jumped out of his vehicle and proceeded up the steps onto the veranda. He slipped off his gumboots at the door, and wandered into the bar. "I'll have a pint thanks Ronnie. Something stronger than that nun's water you served me last time, eh?"

"Coming right up city boy, just don't blame me when you fall off your stool."

When Sam was about half way through his pint Ronnie stopped opposite where he was sitting. "Any sign of your mate today?"

"Nah," Sam said, shaking his head. "I've been down Serpentine Creek."

"Down Serpentine eh? You not bothering with Burke Road anymore?"

"Not at the moment ... figured I'd check a few other spots out while the weekend hunters are out blasting up the countryside."

"Probably a good idea. You look a bit of a bunny, so it's easy to see how a hunter might make a mistake."

"Easy there carrot top," Sam said with a grin.

Ronnie continued wiping the bar. "Check out the beach along Bold Head Road next time you're down that way. I found some nice greenstone there a few years back."

"As long as I find some jade and don't get shot at, I'll be a happy man."

Chapter 14 - Sunday Evening

Decision made, Lydia snagged a dining chair on her way to the bedroom. In the cupboard over the wardrobe, were the suitcases she and Mr G had used when they went to Europe. She climbed up onto the chair, grabbed the bags, and tossed them onto the bed.

Next, she methodically folded her clothes, and packed shoes and other personal items neatly away. There wouldn't be enough room for all her clothes in the two bags, so she threw anything she planned to leave behind in a heap on the floor.

She only allowed herself one pair of stilettos. If she ever made it to Paris, she could buy all the shoes she wanted. In the meantime, she was going to be on the run, her first priority had to be sensible and comfortable clothing, clothes for whatever situation she might find herself in.

For part of the morning, she read the black book, studying its contents. As she prepared for her departure, she found her eyes straying to the cash in the safe. At one point she opened one of the boxes and pulled out a few of the coins, testing their weight in her hand and imagining what she could buy, and where she could go with the money they would bring.

Late in the afternoon, she logged on to the net and checked sailing times for the Bluebridge Ferry south to Picton the next morning. Then, she distributed the gold, and all but one bundle of cash, between the two bags. Despite feeling dirty every time she touched it, the black book and CD went into her handbag for safekeeping, along with the last bundle of banknotes.

As she packed, thoughts of Mr G tracking her down made her palms sweat so much she had to keep wiping them on her pants. But as frightened as she was, now that the decision had been made to take the money, at least she could focus on the job at hand. At one point, she considered leaving a big mess behind. Maybe she'd write 'fuck you' in lipstick on the wall, and chop up his suits. But what was the point?

Besides, if she left the place spotless, Mr G could well think she'd done as he suggested and moved into a serviced apartment or motel somewhere. It might buy her some time if the place looked undisturbed, as if she'd taken everything she owned when she left, and not just packed two bags and skipped town. Who knew how long it would be before he opened the safe again.

Under the kitchen sink, she found an unopened packet of black plastic rubbish bags. Into those, she stuffed everything she wasn't taking with her to the South Island. This tactic might only buy her a day or two before Mr G noticed the missing money, but those days could make all the difference. She had to think smart and use every resource at her disposal if this was going to work.

Five rubbish bags, filled to bursting point, were taken down to the parking garage and dumped into a high-sided bin. Just before the last bag went in she ripped a hole in its side and retrieved a couple of travel brochures depicting the sites of Paris. She'd leave one tucked into the yellow pages in the travel section and another on the floor under the edge of the bed where Mr G could see it when he was standing in the bathroom. Both had to be placed strategically so he didn't suspect they'd been planted. Her going to Paris would seem logical to Mr G, and she most likely would at some time in the future. But right now, she just needed to put him off her trail. Her real trip to Paris would have to wait.

By the time Lydia had everything packed and the apartment cleaned, a big yellow moon had risen over the Miramar Peninsula.

She laid her travel clothes for the next day on the bedroom chair, and put her most comfortable walking shoes on the floor beside them. Her cell phone and laptop were put on their respective chargers.

Once all her preparations were finished, she undressed and snuggled in under the duvet. For a long while, she lay there with her eyes open, looking out at a view she loved so much, knowing she would never see it again. Tomorrow, she would take a step that would forever alter her life one way or another.

Chapter 15 - Monday Afternoon

Mr G tossed his door key into the silver tray on the sideboard, and looked around the apartment. The place looked much the same as when he'd left. If anything, it was tidier. The books that normally sat on the table, by Lydia's favourite chair near the window, were the only things he could see that were missing. Her apartment key, as requested, was sitting on the kitchen bench.

He carried his bag into the bedroom and opened the wardrobe. His clothes hung down at one end. The rest of the room-length rail was empty. The shoe racks on the floor, once filled to overflowing, now held four pair of men's business shoes and a pair of joggers. He'd forgotten how empty his closet had been before Lydia moved in.

Mr G laid his overnight bag on the bed, and tossed a plastic bag of dirty laundry into the hamper. The rest he put away. Once the overnight bag was empty he dumped it on the floor of the wardrobe and looked around the room once more.

Lydia's absence was most noticeable in the bathroom where, for the first time in months, he could see the entire top of the vanity, and not a single undergarment hung on the heated towel rail. He popped his toothbrush in the holder and what few toiletries he had in the top drawer before walking back into the lounge.

Mr G stopped at the sideboard, poured himself a large brandy from the crystal decanter, and took it to the chair by the window to watch the last of the sunset.

His trip to Auckland had been a success. He'd replaced Ethan with an experienced woman recommended by a business colleague. He'd also sought information regarding Ethan's current location, letting it be known that news of his whereabouts would be handsomely rewarded.

Jimmy would collect Ethan's debt plus added expenses once they located him. Mr G didn't really care how Jimmy accomplished the recovery. If Jimmy beat it out of him, so be it.

Ethan deserved whatever he got.

Mr G knew Ethan wouldn't be able to stay away from the casino for long. A couple of weeks and he'd be back throwing money away. His eyes in Auckland would keep him informed of Ethan's return to the tables. He had no doubt he would get his money back. It just might take a little more time, and a few more pints of Ethan's blood before it happened.

As the last of the afternoon light shone through the window, Mr G turned to look at his prized possession sitting on its plinth of black granite. The silver Mercedes glittered like gold as it reflected the pinks and reds now dominating the sky. Then, as the light changed angle slightly, he noticed smudges on the plinth.

Mr G put down his drink and moved closer to the display, bending at the waist to keep the light at the right angle to show the marks on the surface of the polished stone. Clear as day, right where one would push to close the front of the hidden compartment, was a small handprint.

*****

Lydia had tied up her long hair. Sunglasses hid much of her face. She planned to pay cash for everything. When reading the information on the 'how to disappear' websites, she'd noted the importance of not leaving a paper trail. Using a credit card or her real name, would make tracking her far too easy for the trained professionals Mr G would to hire to find her.

When she arrived at the Picton ferry terminal, she'd booked a seat on a shuttle-van to take her south to Christchurch. The shuttle only sat eight people, which suited her fine. The less people she had contact with at this early stage of her disappearance the better. The driver took her money without asking her name, and put her suitcases in the luggage trailer attached to the back of the van.

"Feel free to jump in and wait. We'll leave in about 10 minutes. There's a 15 minute toilet break in Kaikoura. All things going to plan, we should be in Christchurch by 10:00

p.m."

Once in Christchurch, she'd book herself a seat on the first shuttle to Queenstown the following morning, and find a motel.

It would have been quicker to fly, but airlines require ticket holders to show photo I.D. prior to boarding. They also listed passenger's names on a manifest, which would give her pursuers her destination should they be able to access the airline's database somehow. It wasn't worth the risk. Lydia figured it was far better to pay cash for a bus ticket and keep her name out of the computers.

The trip south along the Kaikoura coast went without incident. She loved the cute little motor camp at Waipapa Bay tucked up against the limestone cliffs, its brightly coloured crayfish shop and picnic tables set among fishing nets and floats. She even got a view of the seals at the Oahu Point colony, a few kilometres further south, as the van slowed to negotiate its way around the steep promontory. Evidence of previous rock falls made Lydia nervous as the van twisted along the winding road, but then a couple of minutes later, they were back on the flat, barrelling along the straights into Kaikoura at 100k.

Lydia sat at the back of the van, not wanting to engage with the other passengers. During the drive, she thought about ways of getting her newly acquired wealth into an account she could draw on overseas. After a while, she pulled a paperback out of her bag and tried to read, but found she couldn't concentrate. Later, after a failed nap, she browsed through some of the accommodation brochures the driver kept in the van.

By the time the shuttle pulled into its Christchurch, she had already made a phone booking with a motel a short cab ride from the shuttle van's depot. Perfect, as the next leg of her journey to Queenstown would leave at 9:00 a.m. the next morning.

*****

As soon as the safe popped open Mr G's upper lip twisted into a snarl and a low growl emanated from his reddening face. "You fucking bitch Lydia! I'll bloody well have you for this!"

Mr G bent down in front of the metal box. The only things remaining in the safe were the three ring-binders. The diary, the cash, and the two boxes of gold coins were all gone.

Mr G slammed the safe closed and went to the sideboard to refill his glass.

"How the hell ...?" Mr G mumbled, before taking a large gulp.

Lydia stealing his money was bad enough, but if word got out that he'd lost the diary and the CD, the missing cash and gold coins would be the least of his worries. If those he'd blackmailed found out he no longer had evidence of their indiscretions, they'd become sworn enemies out for revenge. And he'd be helpless to stop them. They would create a tangle of regulatory and financial problems that would tie him up in court for years. Payback would be a bitch, of that he had no doubt.

After slamming his empty glass down, Mr G pulled out his phone and dialled Lydia's number. It was no longer in service. Not surprising really. Had he been in her position, he would have bought a new sim card too.

"Fucking bitch!"

Mr G took a couple of deep breaths and dialled another number.

"Sam is that you?"

"Mr G?" Sam said pulling to the side of the road. "You're lucky you rang when you did, I'm in Runanga. I was just about to go out of cell phone range."

"Runanga? Where the hell is that?"

"Down on the West Coast of the South Island."

"Well fuck the West Coast. I need you back in Wellington ASAP. I've got a major problem."

"Lost another car?" Sam said. His cheeks bunching as he tried not to laugh.

Mr G missed the sarcasm. "Worse, I've had one of my safes

cleaned out. How does your normal rate plus a 10% success bonus on completion sound?"

"It sounds like I'll be driving north as soon as I can get packed." Sam glanced at his watch. "I should make it just in time to catch the 11:00 p.m. ferry."

"Good, come to my office first thing tomorrow morning and I'll fill you in on the details."

*****

The drive up to Picton was one of Sam's favourites. After a quick stop at the cottage to pack, he pulled onto the main road and put his foot down as he headed north.

He noticed the dog-man's white truck sitting in the driveway outside the rented house as he thundered past at 110kph. The turnoff to Burke Road flashed past three kilometres later as he hugged the coast past Punakaiki and on towards Westport before turning inland.

After having a quick bite to eat in Murchison, Sam jumped into the Toyota ready to continue north when his cell phone rang. It was Tane.

"Hiya Sammy boy. I've got the details of that rego you gave me."

"Excellent. Anything unusual?"

"No, nothing. The truck belongs to a Barry Martin from Christchurch. No police record, not even a parking ticket."

"Okay, mate thanks for that. I'll catch you for a beer sometime soon."

Sam disconnected the call and started his vehicle. Once he crossed the bridge leading out of town, he put his foot down.

It wasn't long before he was winding his way through the beautiful native bush of the Buller Gorge. As he drove, he thought about the man with the dog. Not having a record didn't necessarily mean the man wasn't dangerous. It could just mean he was careful.

Sam also wondered how much Mr G had lost from his safe. The money had to be dodgy. Otherwise he would have called the police rather than hire Sam to find it. But that's not what really worried Sam. Stolen property could always be found and recovered. The real question was, who had balls big enough to steal money from Mr G? And even more critical to his wellbeing ... what were they prepared to do to hang on to it?

Just as the light faded, Sam turned east onto State Highway 63 for the relatively straight run through the farmland and vineyards alongside the Wairau River into Blenheim. By 9:30 p.m. he'd turned north again for the thirty minute run up to the ferry terminal in Picton.

When Sam finally saw the lights of Picton up ahead, he breathed a sigh of relief. He'd been behind the wheel for over five hours, and was starting to feel its effects.

After joining the queue of vehicles waiting to board the ferry, he popped into the terminal, paid for his ticket, got a large takeaway coffee, and went back to his vehicle to wait.

Sam stood on deck as the ferry passed through Tory Channel some time later, the calm waters of the Marlborough Sounds giving way to a four meter swell running in Cook Straight. When the ship hit the first trough, both the ferry and Sam's stomach lurched. It would be a long couple of hours before they reached the shelter of Wellington Harbour.

A number of times on the crossing, the ferry dug its prow deep into the oncoming sea, shuddering as over 22,000 tons of steel met a solid wall of water, the resulting spray shooting high into the air, before falling like rain on deck.

When the ferry finally backed into its berth on the outskirts of Wellington, Sam was aching to get off. The trip across Cook Straight had been uncomfortable to say the least. He'd spent much of the trip tucked out of the wind behind a bulkhead on deck, ready to lurch to the railing and ralph his dinner into the ocean.

When the call came over the intercom for passengers to go down to the vehicle deck and prepare to disembark, he smiled for the first time since leaving the calm of the Marlborough Sounds. He couldn't wait to have a hot shower and a good night's sleep in his own bed.

As much as he liked his jaunts down south, there was always something special about coming home to his own space, back to the familiar and comfortable environment he'd created. Not that he'd have long to enjoy it if the urgency in Mr G's voice was anything to go by.

As he drove through town and up the Brooklyn hill towards home, Sam speculated once again about Mr G's dilemma. What would tomorrow bring? Who would he be hunting down this time?

Chapter 16 - Tuesday Morning

Despite getting home late, Sam woke up early by habit. He made himself a cup of coffee, and walked out onto the deck where he could see the sun coming up behind the hills near the airport. Towards the south, the Inland Kaikoura's rose in a purple haze from the blue waters of Cook Strait, patches of snow dusting their tops.

He went into his office, checked his email, and did a little more research on Mr G's business interests. Sam wanted to be prepared for his meeting. Surprises in his line of business were rarely a good thing.

At 8:45 a.m. he grabbed his sunglasses and headed towards the Toyota. The drive down the hill to town would take him ten minutes at most. Finding a car park near Mr G's office once he got there could be another matter altogether.

He said a silly little prayer to the Parking Angel as he searched the narrow city streets. Then, just as he neared Mr G's building, a car indicated its intention to pull out.

"Parking Angel one, traffic nil," Sam said pulling into the vacated spot with a chuckle. "I love it when that happens."

After locking the vehicle and feeding the meter, he wandered into Mr G's building, looking forward to seeing Lydia. Unfortunately, when he arrived at Mr G's suite of offices, the reception area was empty.

"Bugger," he mumbled, disappointed at not seeing the lovely brunette behind the desk. "Knock, knock. Anyone home?"

"Back here Sam, come on through."

Mr G stood when Sam entered the office and waved him towards one of the chairs opposite his desk. "Please sit."

Sam did as he was asked, then looked at Mr G with eyebrows raised. "So you've got some more work for me?"

"Unfortunately yes, and it's a tad delicate. Are you prepared to keep what I tell you confidential?"

"Absolutely. But I reserve the right to turn the job down if I don't like what I hear."

"Fair enough," Mr G said, before taking a seat and opening up the manila folder on his desk. "It's that bitch Lydia."

"Lydia?"

"Yes. I told her I wanted her out of the apartment before I got back from my business trip to Auckland yesterday afternoon. She's moved out alright, but the bitch has cleaned out the contents of my safe at the same time."

"Lydia? Your PA?"

"Yes my thieving fucking PA. Thing is, apart from a stack of cash and some gold coins, she's taken a diary and a CD which contain information I want back."

"And I take it, like last time, you don't want the police involved?"

"Look Sam," Mr G said, "I don't really give a fuck if you approve of me and what I do or not, I just need you to find Lydia."

"What happens when I do?"

"That doesn't concern you. Just tell me where she is and your job is done. It's that simple."

Sam didn't like the sound of what Mr G was inferring. He could understand the man being angry at the theft of his valuables, but Sam knew Mr G's reputation and what he was capable of. It didn't bode well for Lydia.

Mr G stared hard in Sam's direction. "Look Sam, I will find her one way or the other. Do you want the job or should I find someone else?"

Sam didn't really want the job, but at least if he managed to locate her, he could try to negotiate a deal so Lydia didn't get hurt. If Mr G hired another contractor, she may not be so lucky.

"Okay. I'm in. I'll need five grand up front for expenses and as many details as you got — her bank statements, phone records, anything at all however insignificant."

"I'm way ahead of you." Mr G pushed the manila folder across the desk. "I've made a list of friends and family and taken photocopies of the last three months phone account from the apartment and circled all the numbers she's called. There's also a copy of her CV from when she applied for her job here at my office. Oh and a travel brochure I found under the bed in the apartment. The thieving cow always did like Paris."

Sam reached for the folder. "Sounds like a start. I'll get going with this and give you a call if there is anything else."

"Okay. My private number is written inside. You've already got my cell."

Sam stood. "There's just one last thing."

"And that is?"

"A current photo if you've got one."

Mr G reached into his desk drawer and pulled out a snapshot of Lydia standing in front of the Eiffel Tower with a big grin of her face. "Here you go, take this. I don't want it anymore."

Sam turned the photo over in his hand and looked at Lydia's lovely smile before putting it in the folder with the other information. He just hoped he found her first. Otherwise she may not be smiling much in the future.

Chapter 17 - Tuesday Evening

Even though it was 8:00 p.m. by the time the shuttle pulled into Queenstown, it would remain light outside for a while yet. Being less than a month to go before the longest day, sunsets came late this far south.

Once the driver offloaded Lydia's bags, she flagged down a passing taxi and directed them to the small hotel she'd booked up in Sunshine Bay, overlooking Lake Wakatipu and the Remarkables.

Her room had a small balcony with views down the lake. Down the hill towards town, the T.S.S. Earnslaw, a restored steamship complete with white topsides, red funnel, and teak decks, puffed at its berth ready to depart for its evening cruise.

Pleased to be here at last, Lydia lay back on the bed and relaxed. It had been an exhausting couple of days, and she looked forward to a long hot soak and a sleep in.

She'd had lots of time to think while she'd been travelling. One thing she wanted to do before she disappeared for good, was to warn Sam about Mr G's plans to cheat him at cards. Lydia opened up her laptop and logged on to the hotel's network before searching the online white pages for Sam's phone number. Once she'd located it, she pulled her cell phone out of her bag.

After five rings, Sam's answerphone kicked in.

"Hi Sam, this is Lydia. Remember me? I used to work for Mr G. Anyway, I don't work for that bastard any more, but I thought you'd like to know I overheard him talking about some guy he's got coming down from Auckland to cheat you at the next poker game ... just wanted you to know. Good luck."

She hung up and lay down on top of the bedspread, wishing Sam was here, holding her. She'd never felt so alone, or so uncertain of her future. She fluctuated from being terrified one moment, to being excited by the sudden wealth in her possession the next.

At least here in Queenstown a new face didn't make people

look sideways. The town thrived on outsiders. The summer season was steaming ahead, just like the old steamship making its way up the lake.

*****

After Sam left Mr G's that morning, he spent the rest of the day checking out the various short stay accommodation places and travel agents to see if he could pick up Lydia's trail.

Sam used the time honoured principal of eliminating the obvious before complicating matters. Not that he considered Lydia stupid or predictable. Still, he never ceased to be amazed at how many people took the easy option when in flight. They didn't realise that a motel receptionist, even when trying to maintain a guest's privacy, would give away information by their facial expression when shown a photograph and asked direct questions by an experienced investigator. This time however, after a day of searching, Sam had come up empty.

When he got home, he had a hot shower and was about to cook himself some sausages and eggs when he noticed the red light on his answer phone blinking. He pushed the button to retrieve his messages.

"You have one new message. Message received at eight forty eight p.m."

"Hi Sam, this is Lydia. Remember me? I used to work for Mr G. Anyway, I don't work for that bastard any more but I thought you'd like to know I overheard him talking about some guy he's got coming down from Auckland to help cheat you at the next poker game ... just wanted you to know. Good luck."

"Mr G, you festering pile of dog's vomit," Sam mumbled as he hit the replay button to listen to Lydia's message again.

As he listened to the message a second time, he heard a faint tooting in the background, a bit like a steam whistle. He turned up the volume and listened to the message once again.

This time he had no doubt. It was a steam whistle alright. But where would there be one of those? The only steam whistles he'd ever heard, were both in Central Otago.

The first was the Kingston Flyer, a steam locomotive that ran between Frankton and Kingston along the shore of Lake Wakatipu. The second was the T.S.S. Earnslaw, a vintage steamship that operated out of Queenstown.

Sam scratched his head. Then he remembered the paddle steamer operating on the Whanganui River, and the railway museum in Paekakariki that had a restored steam loco.

He jumped onto the internet to have a look, and discovered the Whanganui River cruises only operated during the day, and the steam train at Paekakariki only operated on weekends. Nothing else came up.

From the time of the message, Sam calculated that the whistle had to come from the Earnslaw out on its evening cruise. Nothing else fit. Sam fondly remembered going for a cruise on the still waters of the lake the last time he'd been in Queenstown, it was the first time he'd been on a boat and hadn't felt queasy.

If the tooting on the answer phone message was the Earnslaw, his search for Lydia may only take a day or two rather than weeks or months he'd envisioned.

"Shit that was too bloody easy," Sam said, unsure if he should be impressed with his own skills of deduction or worried about Lydia's simple mistake.

With a good idea of where Lydia was hiding out, now he just needed to work out how to get Mr G's stuff back, and how to keep Lydia safe without getting himself in the shit at the same time.

He figured the best way to do that involved a trip south.

Chapter 18 - Wednesday Morning.

Sam booked himself on the 11:00 a.m. flight out of Wellington. Although he was 99 percent sure Lydia had called him from Queenstown, he still had a bit of work to do. Apart from covering a large area, The Queenstown District also had hundreds of places that provided accommodation, ranging from cabins at the motor camp to luxury five-star boutique hotels. Lydia had enough money to stay pretty much wherever she liked. She could even decide to go further afield to Arrowtown or Glenorchy.

On the two hour flight down the length of the country, Sam spent his time looking out of the window and thinking about how to proceed. If Lydia had been smart enough to figure out how to get into Mr G's safe, she was probably smart enough to pay cash as she went. To use her credit card would have been stupid. So, assuming she was paying cash, she'd probably choose a place that wasn't super expensive. Flashing lots of cash around would seem suspicious, and that would be the last thing she'd want.

Sam thought about what he'd do if he had a stack of stolen cash and gold coins. After some consideration, he figured he'd probably choose a mid-priced place that was private, on the outskirts of town, and had its own restaurant. Queenstown also had two casinos. Lydia could be planning to launder the stolen cash through them by buying chips and then asking for a cashier's cheque when she cashed in. If she kept her bets small, and changed tables frequently, she could gradually exchange cash for chips without attracting the attention of the pit bosses. Sure she might lose somewhere between five and seven percent in the process because of the odds being stacked the house's favour, but that would be small consideration under the circumstances.

Once she had cheques issued by the casino, she could bank them into various overseas accounts without any problem providing she kept transactions under $10,000.

But would Lydia know that? Maybe she wasn't that clever. Maybe she'd just go on a spending spree until the money ran out. She wouldn't be the first thief to take that route. Despite not knowing her all that well, his gut told him she wasn't that silly.

After all, she'd taken the time to call and warn him about Mr G's plan to cheat him at cards. One thing Sam had discovered while tracking down a variety of people over the years was that the more ignorant a person was, the less concern they generally had for others. Using that logic, if Lydia was stupid, she wouldn't have phoned to warn him.

Therefore, if she wasn't stupid, what could have driven her to do something as dangerous as stealing from Mr G?

Whatever Lydia had planned, he was willing to bet big bucks he wouldn't be the only one hunting for her. The look he'd seen in Mr G's eyes was that of a very angry and determined man. Mr G could easily afford to have a number of people looking for his run-away ex.

If Mr G had hired another investigator, Sam also knew his head start wouldn't last long, especially considering the network the brothel owner had at his disposal.

Sam hated to think what Jimmy or some other thug would do if they were first to lay their hands on Lydia. She wouldn't know what hit her. She'd end up being pushed into an ice-cold lake, or under a passing tour bus faster than a falling bungee jumper.

As the flight neared Christchurch, the pilot adjusted the plane's course to the southwest. The terrain below rose to meet them as they flew inland towards the towering peaks of the Southern Alps. When the plane started bouncing on thermals of hot air rising up the sides of the slopes below, Sam swallowed, and dug his fingers into the seat's armrests.

Around 2:00 p.m., after a bumpy ride over Central Otago, the seatbelt sign went on, and they began their descent into Queenstown.

A shimmering heat filled the Wakatipu Basin. The Remarkables looked impossibly high, climbing straight out of the lake, and rising up to touch the few wispy clouds that had lingered past morning. When Sam looked out the plane's window as it banked preparing to line up for its approach, only the deepest and highest valleys still held any trace of the snow that would cover these peaks in winter.

The landing was unspectacular. After picking up his bag and making his way out of the terminal, Sam jumped into a waiting taxi for the fifteen minute journey into Queenstown proper.

"Just drop me off somewhere near the centre of town thanks driver."

Sam sat back and enjoyed the ride from the airport along the Frankton arm of the lake. New developments had sprung up since the last time he was here, creeping further and further up the slopes of Queenstown Hill on the prime land overlooking the lake. On the far side of the water, the Kelvin Heights Golf Course seemed unnaturally green against its arid and rocky backdrop.

Finally the cab crossed the historic stone bridge by the old post office and pulled up to the curb. Sam passed the driver a couple of notes.

"Keep the change."

Seeing the trip was on Mr G, Sam didn't have any reason to skimp on expenses. Especially now that he knew of his employer's plan to cheat him.

Sam sat for a few minutes on one of the benches in the mall, enjoying the sunshine and the dry Central Otago heat. People were everywhere. Most were in groups of two or more, some in groups as large as twenty. The adventure tour booking office had queues of tourists lined up on the footpath, most wearing the standard uniform of tramping boots, shorts, and bush shirts.

It wasn't difficult to pick out the tourists from what they wore, their accents, or their excited behaviour. 'Loopies', the locals called them. Based on some of the things Sam had seen them do on previous trips down this way, it was a nickname that suited them.

After people watching for fifteen minutes or so, Sam figured he's better check in to his accommodation and get to work. The mid-priced room he'd booked, in a small complex near the edge of the lake, was about ten minutes' walk from town. Once he got himself settled, he'd start his hunt in earnest.

Once he'd checked into his room, he took Lydia's photo from the file and did a tour of the main hotels in town. Doing this on foot was far easier than hiring a car. Parking had never been easy in the compact town centre. A hire car would come later if he needed to expand his search.

By 6:00 p.m., he was getting a little hungry from all the walking, so stopped at a cafe for a bite to eat before starting his search again. By the time the light began to fade he'd checked over twenty establishments in the central city area with no luck.

Sam went back to his room for a shower and to rethink his strategy. As he dried himself off, he decided to check out one of the casinos. If his theory about Lydia trying to convert the cash into cashier's cheques was correct, by waiting at the casino, she might well come to him rather than him having to find her. He might even find a game of poker to sit in on while he waited to see if she turned up.

*****

Lydia spent much of the day in her room, or on her balcony resting and reading. She had a light lunch in the hotel's restaurant, and used the spa pool to soak her travel-weary muscles.

When she wasn't reading, she was considering her options. She had looked through the folder of 'local attractions' the hotel provided in each room, and discovered the town had two casinos. She remembered reading about how criminals laundered money in casinos. Maybe this would be an option for her too.

Before she got dressed to go out, Lydia turned on her laptop and Googled 'money laundering'. Wikipedia came up on top of the list, and gave a pretty clear example of how it worked.

The main thing was to make sure she kept any transactions below $10,000 so the casino wasn't legally obligated to report them to the gaming authority.

Lydia was pleased that she'd decided to bring a pair of stilettos and her little black dress with her. Maybe she'd make a night of it, have some fun, and play the tables for a while. A couple of glasses of champagne would go down a treat, all in the name of research of course.

Yes, after dinner she'd wander down into town and check it out. She could scope out the casino's operation, and test her luck at the same time.

Chapter 19 - Wednesday Night

Sam put on a pair of dark blue chinos, light blue shirt, and charcoal merino jersey before checking himself in the mirror. Satisfied he'd blend in with the casino crowd, he left his room, crossed the street, and entered the municipal gardens on the lake's edge. The walk along the shore of Lake Wakatipu into town was a pleasant one. Clear skies and a nearly full moon made navigation easy. The light breeze off the lake had a chill in it making Sam pleased he'd worn warm clothing.

When he reached the casino, his eyes scanned the sparsely populated room for any sign of Lydia. He knew the odds of her being here were slim. He'd used up most of his luck when he got the call that led him to Queenstown in the first place. For her to be in the casino the first time he walked through the door would have required extraordinary luck.

Still, he believed in making his own luck.

Once he'd had a quick check to make sure Lydia wasn't hiding behind one of the rows of slot machines, Sam joined a poker table in the far corner of the room. He chose a seat that gave him a good view of the entrance, yet was semi-obscured by the dealer sitting on the opposite side of the table. Hopefully, Lydia wouldn't spot him if she came in.

The stakes on the table were modest so he could play and watch at the same time without the fear of losing too much money through inattention. With a little luck, he might even make a few extra bucks while he waited.

After sitting down, Sam dropped two $100 notes onto the table in front of him. The dealer converted the bills to chips, and Sam settled in to play while keeping his eye on the door.

Sam's father had taught him how to play tight poker, so after the first hour he had won a small amount despite the casino's rake. He hadn't been involved in very many hands, but he'd taken down enough pots to keep himself ahead of the game.

After two hours, he was up $130 and just about to cash in

and wander off to see if Lydia had gone to the casino down the street, when he caught a glimpse of a dark-haired woman wearing a body-hugging black dress and high-heels enter the lobby. He leaned slightly to the right, using the dealer as a shield and slumped down in his chair.

The woman had her head turned and was partially hidden by a couple who had come in before her. It looked like Lydia, but he couldn't be sure. The woman walked over to the bar, sat on a stool, and ordered a drink. When her glass arrived, she swivelled her stool around to view the room as she took a sip.

"Bingo."

"Sir?" The dealer asked Sam.

"Oh nothing ... sorry."

Sam held his hand up to his forehead, partially covering his eyes. He felt exposed sitting here in plain sight, so he thanked the dealer and picked up his chips before sneaking around behind a bank of poker machines. There he found an unoccupied seat that allowed him a narrow view between two machines to where Lydia sat at the bar. From this position, he could watch comfortably without there being much chance of her catching sight of him.

After sipping her wine for a few minutes, Lydia moved to a roulette table. She withdrew some cash from her purse and placed it on the table, receiving two stacks of purple chips in return.

Sam played the minimum amount of credits as slowly as possible on his pokie as he watched Lydia at the roulette table. She seemed to be holding her own, betting black 90 percent of the time. The male players at the table had perked up since her arrival, but that didn't surprise Sam. After all, she was an attractive woman.

After watching Lydia play for fifteen minutes or so, Sam noticed something unusual. The floor manager stopped for a chat with the pit boss, which was not unusual in itself. However, when the floor manager nodded in Lydia's direction, and pulled what looked like a photograph from his top pocket to show to the pit boss, Sam immediately realised that Mr G's network had swung into action. He must have circulated Lydia's picture to the casinos already.

After a few more words, the floor manager left the pit boss and started to walk towards a couple of men in black suits standing near the cashier's cage on the far side of the room.

Sam had to think fast. Thankfully, the man sitting next to Lydia was in the process of gathering his chips and vacating his seat, so Sam circled around behind Lydia, and as soon as the man stood up, he squeezed into his place.

"Lydia, listen to me," Sam whispered. "We don't have much time."

As Lydia turned, her eyes widened. "Sam? Wha ...what are you doing here?"

"I don't have time to explain. Please just trust me when I say we need to get out of here right now. Mr G must have circulated your picture to all the casinos."

"But how, how did you ...?"

Sam looked Lydia straight in the eyes. "Look, I'll explain when we're safe. Trust me. Put your chips in your bag and stand up."

Sam could tell Lydia was confused but when he took her elbow and stood, she rose from her seat as well. "But ..."

"Please Lydia, we have to go right now." Sam said with as much urgency as he could without yelling. "Take my arm and start walking towards the door."

Sam breathed a sigh of relief when Lydia dropped her chips into her handbag and hooked her arm through his, allowing him to lead her at a reasonable pace towards the door.

Just as they entered the lobby, Sam heard footsteps on the tiles behind them.

"Hey you two. Stop!"

Sam's hand found Lydia's and he increased his pace as they skipped past the slow to respond doorman. Unsure of what to do, and hesitant to leave his designated post, the doorman looked towards the floor manager for instruction. His hesitation was just the break Sam and Lydia needed.

Being tourist season, the Queenstown streets were crowded

with people. Sam and Lydia zigzagged through a group of boisterous diners exiting the restaurant next door, and ducked down a narrow alley that ran through to the mall.

"Quickly this way," he said, still holding Lydia's hand and tugging her along.

By the time the floor manager got outside, Sam and Lydia were nowhere to be seen.

They returned to Sam's room by a circuitous route, making sure none of the men from the casino were in pursuit.

"Come on, I've got a room here, we need to get off the street, then I'll explain."

Wondering how she'd been found so soon, Lydia realised she had little choice but to do what Sam suggested. If Sam could find her, so could others. At least she had a good feeling about Sam, unlike most of Mr G's associates she'd had the misfortune to meet.

Sam took one last look in both directions, swiped his key card and opened the door to his room.

Lydia sat down on the edge of the bed, took off her shoes, and massaged her toes. "These shoes were not designed for running. Now, would you please tell me what the heck is going on?"

Even before Sam had finished explaining things, she knew she was in deep trouble.

Lydia hid her eyes behind her hand as she slumped down, resting her elbow on one knee. She shook her head back and forth a moment and then looked up at Sam standing by the door. "So what now?"

Sam eyes tilted skyward as he shrugged. "That is a very good question." He took two steps, opened up the fridge, and pulled out a beer. "You want something to drink while I think this through?"

"Any bubbles in there? God I'm shaking."

He located a small bottle of Lindauer in the door of the fridge, poured some into a glass, and handed it to Lydia. "There you go."

He pulled a straight chair out from under the table, and took a seat facing her. "Now tell me, what in God's name possessed you to steal from a man like Mr G? Have you got a death wish or something?"

Lydia fidgeted on the edge of the bed, blushed, and took another gulp of wine. "He kicked me out. I figured I'd hide out down here for a while until I sorted a way to skip the country. How in hell did you find me so quickly?"

Sam explained to her about hearing the steam whistle on her message. "Once I was in Queenstown, checking the casino made sense."

This information made Lydia realise what a rank amateur she was. What a fool she'd been to think she could hide in a country as small as New Zealand.

"I suspected Mr G would have others looking ... seems I was right. You're just lucky you warned me with that phone call, otherwise Mr G's men would have grabbed you, and you'd be locked in a back office right now waiting for him to arrive."

Lydia wrapped her hands around her upper arms and shivered. Sam picked up the bottle of Lindauer, and topped up her glass. After taking a gulp, Lydia peered up at Sam with moist eyes. "So what now?"

"Well having to scarper from the casino like that wasn't quite the smooth operation I had planned." Sam said looking at a still trembling Lydia. "I was hoping to find you and negotiate a settlement that would keep you safe before Mr G knew where you'd gone. God knows what he'll do now that we've lost our leverage. There are only a couple ways out of this town you know."

"Will you help me? I—I just made a silly mistake. I'll give him back his filthy money."

"First of all, I should probably give him a call and see if I can sort this mess out. I'm assuming you've got the contents of the safe here in Queenstown with you."

"Yes it's all locked in my hotel room, apart from these." Lydia pulled the diary and CD out of her handbag and handed them to Sam. "You wouldn't believe some of the things he's got in there."

Sam took the rubber band off the diary and had a flick through its pages.

"Jesus," he said, shaking his head. "It's like a who's who of shady deals."

"I know. You should see the photos on the CD. Most of them are absolutely disgusting."

"Okay, well let's think this through. We'll need to have a clear plan in mind before I make a call and try to broker a deal."

*****

Mr G had just walked into the back office at his club when his cell phone rang. "Yes?"

"Mr G, Bryan Hall from Queenstown."

"Bryan, what can I do for you?"

"That photo you emailed me. I've seen her. She's here in Queenstown."

"Did you get her into holding?"

"Some guy I've never seen before rushed her out of the casino just as my boys were about to grab her. We followed them out onto the street, but they disappeared into the crowd before I could do anything."

"What did this mystery man look like?"

"Tall, lean ... two day stubble, dark hair."

"Sounds like Sam McKee," Mr G said.

How the hell had he found her so quickly? Mr G wondered. He'd told Sam to contact him the minute he had any news. Unless ...

"Hey Bryan, did they come into the casino together?"

"I didn't see them come in, but they were certainly looking pretty friendly when they left."

"Fuck!" Mr G said slamming his fist on the desk. "Look Bryan, I need you to rustle up all the spare muscle you've got and lock Queenstown down. It's critical those two don't leave town without a shadow. Can you do that for me?"

"I think so. The planes don't fly out at night, so it's just the shuttle vans and the rental car outlets we'll need to worry about."

"I doubt they have a car, but it's possible."

"Look I'll get my guys on to it. There are only a couple of roads out of town. I'll get some men posted to keep watch."

"Good. I'll fly down on the first available flight tomorrow morning with my driver. You get going, there's a big bonus for you if you can find them."

Mr G went to a cabinet on the back wall and poured a large brandy before jumping online to book the flights to Queenstown. He arranged it so Jimmy arrived from Auckland an hour before the Wellington to Queenstown flight departed. That way, they could travel down together. Next, he phoned a few of his pals around the South Island, speaking to everyone that might come into play. There was no need to fill them in on too many details, other than the fact that he was looking for two people who'd ripped him off big time. The hefty reward he was offering was a great motivator.

Once he'd alerted everyone he could think of, and had forwarded them each a copy of the photo Bryan had supplied from the casino's security cameras, he locked his office and headed home to pack.

As he walked the three blocks to his apartment, Mr G fondled the knife in his jacket pocket and wondered if Sam had been playing him all along.

Just as he opened his apartment door, the phone rang. He hurried over to snatch up the receiver.

"Yes?"

"Mr G, its Sam McKee. We need to have a word."

"What makes you think I want to talk with you, you traitorous bastard?"

"Now, now, Mr G. No need to be like that."

"Why the fuck didn't you call me the moment you found out Lydia had gone to Queenstown, eh?"

"Look, I was going to call you. I just needed to work things through," Sam said.

"Work what things through? You mean work through how you two could rip me off? My man said you two looked pretty fucking cosy when he saw you running from his casino."

This conversation wasn't going the way Sam had planned. He turned and shook his head at Lydia before trying a different approach. "Mr G, I've called to arrange the return of your property. Isn't that what you want?"

"Don't you worry Sammy boy, I'll get my property back alright, and then I'm going to make sure the lovely Lydia ain't so lovely any more. If you don't want the same treatment, I suggest you frogmarch that thieving cow back down to the casino and hand her and the stolen goods over to the floor manager. He'll keep her on ice until I arrive tomorrow morning.

"You know I can't turn her over to you if I think you're going to hurt her."

"What's your alternative, the police? You seriously think the cops are going to take the word of a pair of thieves over a respectable businessperson like myself. There's nothing linking me with that book. Besides, I've got friends in high places in case you'd forgotten. You'll both spend the next ten years behind bars ... and believe me Sam, I can make sure those ten year are fucking uncomfortable."

Without seeing Mr G's eyes, Sam couldn't tell if he was bluffing. He probably did have contacts that could make life difficult for them.

"Surely the sensible thing is for me to arrange the return of your stuff and call it quits?" Sam tried one more time. "She just made a silly mistake, she realises that now. That way you get your money, and never have to see her again."

"Sam, I'll make you an offer. Give you a chance to prove you weren't in on this. Just take Lydia down to the casino along with my property and I'll let you walk. But there is no fucking way that bitch is getting off without being punished. It would set a bad example for the rest of my crew."

Sam sat in silence, wondering if there was any point in replying.

"You've got one hour. If I don't get a call from Bryan by then, you're a dead man. You hear me Sam? A FUCKING DEAD MAN!"

Sam closed his cell and looked at Lydia. "Houston, we have a problem."

A look of dismay crossed Lydia's face.

"He's gone totally septic. We need a plan B, and we need it fast."

Lydia forced out a smile. "At least money won't be an issue."

"There is that." Sam said, doing his best to sound unafraid. He glanced down at his watch. "Look it's only eleven o'clock. I have an old mate who lives up in Sunshine Bay, just south of town. We used to work at the Mexican restaurant together back in the days when we were both into skiing. I'll ring him and see if he's got a car we can borrow. Best if we get out of town before the noose tightens. Mr G's bound to fly in reinforcements tomorrow."

"But where do we go?"

"Just before Mr G hired me to look for you, I rented a secluded little cottage over on the West Coast for a three week holiday. When I rushed back to Wellington I never did get around to cancelling it. We could head there and hide out until we sort something out."

Lydia was in over her head and she knew it. "It doesn't sound like we've got many other options."

"Okay. Well I'll call Jesse and see what the story is."

A sleepy sounding Texan answered on the fifth ring.

"Hey amigo, it's Sam ... Sam McKee. Sorry to wake you up but I need your help."

Sam explained their need for transportation.

"Jesus Sam, of course you can borrow a car. Why don't you take my old Pajero? Since I bought the Harley, I barely use it these days. Can you catch a cab up here, or do you want me to come and pick you up?"

"I don't think a cab is a good idea, too easy to trace."

It took less than twenty minutes for Jesse to arrive. He

recognised his old friend's Pajero from the many times they'd taken it up to the Coronet Peak ski field. Sam grabbed his bag and went out first. He had a quick look around before waving Lydia out of the room and into the back seat.

"Hey thanks amigo. We just need to make a quick stop on the way back to your place to pick up Lydia's luggage."

When they pulled up outside Lydia's hotel Sam suggested that Jesse wait in the shadows while they collected Lydia's gear.

After tossing Lydia's bags into the back, Sam tried to relax. He turned to look at Lydia. "You okay?"

Lydia shook her head and chewed her lip. "I'll be better when we're out of here."

Sam reached over and gently rubbed her forearm. "Not long now."

Lydia put her hand on top of Sam's. "Thanks for doing this. I realise the risk you're taking."

Sam could see a dog's silhouette in the window of Jesse's dining room when the Pajero pulled into the driveway. Jesse ushered them in. "Don't worry the dog's a sook. He won't bite. But try to be quiet, the wife's asleep. She's got an early shift in the morning."

In the kitchen, Jesse pointed towards a row of stools lined up under a breakfast bar. "Grab a seat … Coffee?"

"I'd love to stay and catch up mate, but we really need to move. I want to be as far from here as possible by morning."

"No worries. I put a few things you may need in the back of the old girl. Water, a few tins of food, an old duvet and some camping stuff, tarp, firelighters, that sort of thing."

Sam grabbed Jesse in a bear hug and slapped his back. "Thanks mate you're a lifesaver … literally."

"Can I give you some money for the use of your truck?" Lydia said. "I don't know when we'll be able to return it."

"Don't be silly, Sam's a mate. Besides, there's no rush. If you have to abandon the old girl somewhere, just stick the key in the magnetic key box attached to the spare wheel bracket and let me know. I'll organise someone to collect it."

Sam motioned to Lydia, "We'd better make a move."

Jesse watched as Sam backed out of the driveway and into the street. With a final wave, the two fugitives drove off down the hill towards the main road out of town.

*****

It had only been an hour, and already Bryan's man was fiddling with the radio and chain-smoking. He'd been told to position himself near the Frankton lights on the edge of town and watch for the two people whose photos sat on the seat beside him. He could have counted the traffic that had gone past on one hand. He'd need to start rationing his ciggies. At the rate he'd been sucking them down, he'd run out before morning.

It had been Matt's night off when Bryan rang, and although annoyed at being disturbed at home, the promised bonus if he managed to spot the two runaways would more than make up for a lost night playing on his Xbox.

As Matt did his best to stay awake, he noticed the headlights of a group of cars, four or five in all, coming in his direction following a campervan.

Typical loopies, he thought. Bastards never pull over and let traffic pass. He was about to start fiddling with the radio again when he spotted a familiar face in the second to last vehicle in the row. He rechecked the photo he'd been given. It was her alright.

He started his engine and pulled out onto the highway, at the same time reaching for his cell phone.

Bryan figured that if these people were prepared to steal from Mr G, stealing a car wouldn't pose much of a moral dilemma, so he'd posted cars on all the roads out of town, one each for Frankton, Arrowtown, and Glenorchy.

It wasn't long before Bryan's phone rang.

"Bryan, it me Matt. They've just passed me in a red Pajero heading towards the Lower Shotover Bridge. "What should I do?"

"Just follow them and let me know when they stop. And for Christ's sake stay back, don't let them see you."

While talking on the phone, Matt had accelerated up to the line of cars. After Bryan's comment, he took his foot off the pedal and dropped back a little, ready to follow wherever the Pajero lead him. At least the drive would give him plenty of time to plan how to spend his bonus.

*****

Sam and Lydia toddled along in the queue of cars behind the slow-moving camper, waiting for an opportunity to pass.

As the parade of vehicles approached the lights at Frankton, Sam noticed an occupied car on the side of the road, a strange place to park this time of night. Thinking it might be a mufti traffic cop he instinctively looked at his speedometer.

"Ha!"

"What's so funny?" Lydia asked.

"That car back there looked like a cop, so I checked my speedo. We're doing exactly 40kph in a 70kph zone. Damn campervans. At this rate it'll take forever to get anywhere."

"Why are they on the road this late anyway?" Lydia asked. "They doing a runner from the campground or something?"

Sam chuckled and checked his mirrors. He saw the parked car they'd just passed pull onto the highway and race up to the line of cars, slowing once it was on the tail of the car ten metres behind him.

Sam's paranoia kicked in. Wondering if Mr G's lookouts were already in place, Sam watched his mirrors. After a minute, the car dropped back and sat 100 metres behind the others, keeping pace with the slow queue of traffic but not really attached to it.

"I think we've picked up a tail. That car that just joined the queue is acting pretty suspiciously."

"Damn," Lydia said. "What do we do now?"

As Sam thought about Lydia's question, he saw a sign that indicated the turnoff to Cadrona and Wanaka via the Crown

Range Road was coming up in two kilometres.

"Hang on I have an idea."

As the line of cars started around a long sweeping left-hand bend, Sam dropped back a bit from the cars in front of him.

"If I remember correctly, there's a big straight just around this corner, if there's no traffic coming the other way I'm going to boot it and slingshot past the whole row in one go."

One hundred metres from the end of the sweeper, Sam put his foot down, building speed as he gained on the slow-moving queue in front of him. When the Pajero rounded the corner, Sam edged out into the oncoming lane to look for traffic. When he couldn't see any headlights, he kept his foot planted to the floor, and tooted his horn to let the other drivers know he was jumping the queue.

The driver of the camper, seeing a straight road and a 100 kph sign ahead, in typical loopie fashion, planted his foot as well, rather than let the other cars pass.

"Dickhead!" Sam cursed as the Pajero started to run out of passing room. By the time he managed to edge the Pajero past the campervan, he was a mere 200 metres from the turnoff.

Fifty metres from the intersection, Sam turned off the Pajero's headlights. Then, like a racecar entering pit lane, without indicating or touching his breaks, he veered left at the junction, coasted uphill and swerved into a parking bay before yanking on the handbrake.

When the Pajero came to a stop, Sam craned his neck around and watched as the rest of the traffic drove on past the turnoff as if nothing was amiss.

"I bet the driver of that campervan is wondering what you've been smoking."

"Sorry about that. I didn't know what else to do. At least this road stays pretty straight as it runs through the Gibbston Valley from here on. With luck, the driver of the campervan will keep his foot down, and whoever was following us will think we're still at the front of the queue. Hopefully, by the time he realises we're gone, we'll be far away."

"Nice trick."

"Providing it works. In the mean time, let's get the hell out of here."

Sam put the Pajero back in gear and stomped on the accelerator, firing a cloud of dust and gravel into the night as they wheel-spun back onto the tarmac and up the steep incline towards Cadrona.

*****

It wasn't until the line of vehicles went around a sharp U-shaped corner some nine kilometres past the Cadrona turnoff that Matt realised the Pajero wasn't in the row of vehicles any more.

"What!" He yelled as he looked for somewhere to turn around. "Where the hell did you go?" Bryan would not be impressed, and Matt knew he'd be in deep trouble if he didn't hurry up and find them again.

When Matt spotted a pull-in bay up ahead he braked sharply into it, spun the wheel and planted his foot, fish-tailing the car around before speeding off in the opposite direction.

"Shit! Shit! Shit!" he said, thumping the steering wheel. He'd be lucky to get anything for his night's efforts now. How had he missed them when they turned off? How had they even known he was following them?

Matt considered calling Bryan, but discounted the idea. With luck, he might manage to locate the Pajero again and avoid having to admit he'd been a fool. Bryan didn't tolerate incompetence. This error could cost him work in the future, and work wasn't that easy to find in Queenstown for someone with his skill set, unless of course, he wanted work for minimum wage washing dishes, tending bar, or unloading bags off tour buses.

But how was he to know which of the many side-roads the Pajero had taken? All the vineyards in this area had access roads intersecting the main highway. The Pajero could have taken any one of them. Every half a kilometre or so along this part of the Gibbston Valley, there'd be another road he'd have to check. Some of them meandered kilometres into the foothills. Even if he managed to find a Pajero parked up somewhere, how could he tell it was the one he was looking for? He hadn't had a chance to make a note of the registration number. Besides, Pajeros were common in a climate where four wheel drive was almost a necessity in winter, especially once the snow came.

As Matt drove back towards Queenstown, he slowed to look down each side road and driveway he came to. It didn't take long before he realised the hopelessness of his task.

"Shit, shit, shit!" Matt screamed out the window. Then he pulled off to the side of the road and opened his phone.

He shook his head as he punched in Bryan's number, mumbling one last "shit" before Bryan answered.

Chapter 20 - Thursday Morning

When Sam reached the top of the first major climb, he pulled over and looked back towards Queenstown. There was no sign of headlights on the mountain road that twisted and turned far below them. This was not a road well travelled at night, with nothing but rocky crags, icy streams, tussock and thorn-covered matagouri for 60 odd kilometres. The next petrol station was a half an hour drive past the Cadrona Village, in Wanaka, assuming it was even open this late.

"Looks like we made a clean getaway … so far anyway."

Lydia turned and looked Sam in the face. "Thank God for that. How long until we get to this hideout of yours?"

"From here it's about six hours. It's just after one now. Why don't you get some sleep? I'll wake you up in a few hours and you can drive for a spell. Can you drive one of these things?"

"I was brought up on a high-country farm," Lydia said with a cheeky grin. "I can drive anything."

It took him a moment to pull his eyes away from Lydia's face. The half shadow made her flawless skin and green eyes even more beautiful.

When he realised he was staring, he dragged his eyes away. "Great. Well you may as well try and get some sleep. I'll do my best not to throw you around."

Lydia didn't need much encouragement. Two days travel, and all the drama of the last few hours, had left her exhausted. She leaned her seat back, and grabbed the duvet Jesse had so thoughtfully provided from the seat behind her, wrapping it around her as she curled up on her side facing Sam.

"Thanks again for helping me. If I'd known you were such a gallant knight I'd have gotten into trouble sooner."

Sam chuckled. "Sleep fair maiden, we've got a big day tomorrow."

*****

162

"What do you mean you've lost them?" Bryan shouted down the phone. "Do you realise what you've done you idiot!"

"I'm sorry boss, but they just disappeared into thin air. I can't understand it."

"Jesus Christ," Bryan said, his hand reaching for his brow as he released a long stream of air through pressed lips. "Okay so where are you now?"

"I'm parked up along the Gibbston Highway."

"Okay, tell me what happened from the very beginning," Bryan said, ducking into his office for some privacy.

Matt told Bryan how, after picking up the Pajero just out of Frankton, he'd tucked himself at the back of the queue so he could follow without attracting suspicion.

"I saw them pass the row of cars but they didn't seem to be pulling away so I just stayed where I was, thinking I'd be less conspicuous. Then, about half way to the Cromwell Gorge, the road curved around this sharp corner and I realised that the Pajero wasn't there anymore."

Bryan pulled the computer keyboard over and brought up Google maps. He zoomed into the area Matt was talking about.

"So the last time you saw them was when they pulled out to pass the row of cars right?"

"Yeah."

"Which side of the Cadrona turnoff was that?"

"I think I was past ... no wait I remember seeing the sign just before he took off."

"So he could have turned up the Crown Range, right?"

"I didn't see any cars turn off."

"But by then you were at the back of the queue and he was at the front."

"Yeah I guess."

"So you don't really know shit do you Matt?"

Matt may have been a meathead, but he was smart enough not to argue.

Bryan looked at his watch. It was nearly 1:15 a.m. "Look he may have turned off almost anywhere. I want you to start searching from where you first noticed he was missing, but do it systematically. Don't miss any side roads. I'll get Jack to start looking from the Queenstown end of the valley. When the two of you meet in the middle, or if you find them, give me a call."

"But that could take all night."

"Well whose stupid fault it that?" Bryan said, before shaking his head and rolling his eyes.

Bryan ended the call and looked at the screen again, trying to work out the possible routes the Pajero could have taken. Towards Wanaka was the most likely. From there they could go over the Haast Pass to the West Coast. That would be as good a place as any to hide out. The other option was towards Cromwell and on to Alexandra. Maybe they'd ducked off the main road and rejoined it at some other point once they'd lost Matt?

Bryan knew people in both of those areas. He just needed to get them mobilised and looking. He started making a list. Some he could phone, but others he'd have to email or text. With luck, they'd picked up their messages by early morning at the latest. He attached a picture from the security camera of the runaways and started firing off messages.

It took Bryan over an hour to get things in place. On the off chance that Sam and Lydia made it that far, Bryan also emailed his old drinking buddy Ronnie, the publican at his favourite drinking establishment on the West Coast. Bryan knew that if anyone was likely to hear of a couple of strangers turning up on the West Coast, it would be Ronnie MacDonald.

*****

The night drive through Mount Aspiring National Park was both eerie and beautiful. As the moon rose, it illuminated patches of late snow high on the peaks. Waterfalls cascaded within view of the road, glistening in the mellow light.

Sam found a place to pull over not long after they had crested the top of the Pass. "Lydia, wake up," Sam said softly, not wanting to startle her. "It's your turn to drive."

Lydia arched her back and had a stretch before opening the

door and walking around to the driver's side of the Pajero.

Once she'd adjusted the seat she looked at Sam. "So where am I going?"

"Just keep following State Highway 6 until we get to Fox Glacier. That should take a couple of hours. Wake me up when we get there okay?"

Lydia nodded and released the handbrake. "You're the boss Sir Galahad."

*****

Mr G was not impressed when Bryan phoned at 3:00 a.m. and told him about Matt's brain fart.

"So you think the most likely scenario is that they've headed northwest towards the West Coast?" Mr G asked.

"One of my contacts is the attendant at the 24-hour petrol station in Wanaka. He said a guy looking like our boy filled up sometime around two. My man didn't notice a woman with him, but said the guy was driving a red 4x4 of some sort. There's not a lot of traffic that time of night so I think there's a fairly good chance it was them."

"Makes sense. Thank Christ you don't have many roads down there. I think I'd better change my flights and see if I can get into Westport instead of Queenstown. I can hire a car and head south from there."

"Good idea. I'll let you know when I hear anything more."

Mr G turned to his laptop and started looking for tickets to Westport. The only flight he could get seats on didn't leave until late morning, but it was still quicker than flying into Christchurch and driving five hours over the Alps or going to Nelson and driving down through the Buller Gorge. Next, he organised one of his associates to have a car waiting for them at the terminal when he and Jimmy arrived.

"Wait till I get my hands on you Lydia," Mr G mumbled, taking another slurp of his brandy. "Even Sam McKee won't be able to save you."

*****

Just on first light, Sam and Lydia left Greymouth, their tank full of diesel, and their eyes full of sleep.

"Not far now. You'll love this place. It rustic, but comfortable in a West Coast sort of way."

"I've never been in this part of the country before. I'm looking forward to having a look."

"Well believe me you're in for a treat."

The two drove in silence for the next fifteen kilometres. They had just passed through the township of Rapahoe when they rounded a corner and the vista opened up before them. Suddenly, as the closeness of the bush released them from its grasp, there was nothing but ocean stretching all the way to the horizon.

"Wow," Lydia said, a huge smile crossing her face. "That's amazing."

As the road swung around to the right and ran parallel to the coast, their view changed. Now they could see the whole coast curving in a gentle arc to the north, its bush-covered hills plunging steeply into the Tasman Sea.

Rocky islands thrust like towers through the crashing waves on one side. While high granite bluffs rose near vertically towards a grey sky on the other. Waterfalls danced and splashed from the saturated cliffs above, and small cascades, their wispy tails caught by the wind, blew across the road, forcing Sam to keep his wipers on despite the rain having stopped over an hour ago.

"Pretty awesome eh?" Sam never tired of this first glimpse of the coast as the full extent of its beauty spread like wings before him. He turned towards Lydia, his eyes sparkling. "It's like a different world over here. This part of the coast is so — so primordial, like taking a big step back in time."

As Lydia surveyed the scene before her, she understood exactly what he meant.

A little further on they reached Ten Mile Creek where the road descended steeply into a fern covered gully before crossing a narrow one-way bridge and climbing up and out the other side, the granite cliffs overhanging the road in parts.

"Not much further now," Sam said.

Every turn they took exposed a gorgeous new vista. Ranks of whitecaps marched towards shore in endless rows, while on the cliff side of the road, masses of moss, ferns and lichens hung from the sheer rock-face, creating fabulous hanging gardens of greens, yellows and rusty reds.

At times, the road would duck inland for a short spell, tunnelling into the overhanging bush, and beech trees, ferns, flaxes, and nikau palms, would crowd the highway for a while. Then, as the highway crested the top of a bluff, a new scene would reveal itself, like turning the page of a calendar to reveal next month's picture.

At the top of one steep stretch of road, Sam pulled into a lookout area and stopped. Far below, the river flats spread before them, an oasis of flatland ringed by mountains and sea.

"That's the Barrytown flats down there," Sam said pointing. "You can almost see the cottage from here. It's just inland from that wee island there."

Lydia took in the scene without speaking, knowing any comment she made would ruin the moment.

After sitting for a couple of minutes, Sam reluctantly put the vehicle in gear and drove off.

Less than ten minutes later, he pulled the Pajero in between the flaxes and came to a stop outside the cottage. "It's not quite the penthouse apartment you're used to, but as far as locations go, you've got to admit it's pretty spectacular."

"It's so cute," Lydia exclaimed, as she opened her door and jumped out of the vehicle. "I feel like I've been transported back to the 70s." She turned and looked at the sea to her left. "My God, look at the size of those waves."

Out towards the island, huge rollers pounded in. Plumes of white spray shooting skyward as blue-grey monsters crashed on the rocks.

"Not many sail in these waters, those waves are the main reason why." Sam opened the back of the Pajero and started hauling their bags out. "The key is under the fourth rock to the right of the door. Do you mind? I'll carry these."

Lydia found the key and Sam lugged her two big bags into the cottage. He put them down between the table and the bed. Next, he grabbed his suitcase, the duvet, and the bag of supplies he'd picked up from the service station while refilling the car in Greymouth.

"I don't know about you but I'm zonked," Sam said with a yawn. "You take the bed. I'll curl up in the armchair."

Lydia turned to Sam. She took a step forward and wrapped her arms around his waist, looking up into his eye. "I hope this doesn't seem too silly, but it's been a stressful couple of days, and I'm still a bit freaked out. Would you mind holding me while we sleep? I'd feel much safer."

"I—I guess that would be okay," Sam said, feeling butterflies in his stomach.

Lydia stood on her tiptoes and pecked Sam on the cheek before dropping back down and giving Sam a cheeky grin. "Are you seeing anyone at the moment?"

"No. Why?"

"Just thought I'd check in case I have an overwhelming desire to touch you when I wake up."

Sam felt heat rise to his face, but he quickly recovered from his surprise. "Well if you do, just make sure I'm awake. I'd hate to miss it."

*****

Ronnie read Bryan's email a second time and then opened the attached image. His eyes widened when a photo of Sam McKee, arm in arm with an attractive woman, popped up on the screen.

How had Sam gotten himself mixed up in this mess? Ronnie looked at the woman again. She had a shapely figure and lovely long hair. He figured this mess was probably her fault. Women were trouble. An otherwise intelligent man could do stupid things around a beautiful woman. He knew that for a fact.

Still, Sam was okay, especially considering he was a city boy. They got on, and the banter was lively. But then that's what a publican did if he wanted to make a living. What he didn't like was Sam finding all the good jade on his beach, especially around Burke Road. That area had been Ronnie's happy hunting ground for a number of years. Although he relied on tourists for his living, jade had become his obsession. When one conflicted with the other, he was torn.

Money was hard to come by on the West Coast, and the reward being offered by Bryan for information leading to the two people in the photograph was substantial. Claiming the reward would not only solve his cash flow problem, but it might also scare Sam off his favourite beach.

Ronnie considered his options for the briefest of moments before reaching for the phone.

"Hey Bryan, Ronnie here."

"Ronnie, so you got my email?"

"Yes, and I know the guy you're looking for. He's was here a few days back doing a bit of jade hunting in the area. He's been in for a drink a couple of times."

"Look, Ronnie, those two left Queenstown last night and are headed your way. Do you know where he stays when he's over there?"

"Not exactly, he mentioned a cottage once, but there's a heap of cribs in the area, he could be any number of places. The best chance to find him might be when he goes looking for jade, or here in the pub."

"Okay, Ronnie, good work. Mr Graeme, the guy who's paying the reward, is driving down from Westport this afternoon. I'll get him to pop into the pub and see you. Tell him everything you know. If this pans out you'll be in for a nice chunk of cash. You'll be there this afternoon won't you?"

"Hey, mate, I'm the publican. The locals would string me up if I wasn't."

"Okay, well keep an eye out. Mr Graeme's about six foot, solid build, face like a boxer. He'll have his driver with him.

Everyone calls him Mr G."

"Mr G. Got it."

"And for fuck sake Ronnie, be respectful. This is one guy you don't want to piss off."

*****

Lydia slept secure in Sam's arms, her head resting on his chest, her breathing long and slow.

Sam, on the other hand, dozed fitfully, waking every twenty minutes or so, staring at the ceiling, wondering when Lydia would wake, and when she did, whether she'd be as friendly as she'd sounded before going to sleep.

As he drifted in and out of sleep, his mind entered that shallow dream state where his imagination floated lightly, flitting from one thing to the next. He imagined how she might touch him, and how he might reciprocate.

At first, when he felt fingertips run lightly across his chest, he wasn't sure if he was still dreaming or not. In either case, it felt nice and he relaxed, sinking further into the sensation.

"You awake?" Lydia said in a whisper, not wanting to disturb Sam if he was still asleep.

"Mmmm ..."

Upon hearing a reply, Lydia's hand crept up to Sam's face and lightly touched the stubble on his chin, before tracing the outline of his lips with her forefinger. Sam's fingers found the soft skin behind Lydia's ear and caressed it gently as Lydia tilted her head upward.

Their lips brushed together softly at first, playful and tender. As their ardour grew, their mouths came together with more passion, lips opening slightly, tongues searching. Lydia turned towards Sam, one of her legs slotted itself between his as she pressed her body against his thigh and abdomen. A soft murmer escaped Lydia's lips as she felt Sam's warmth below her.

Lydia closed her eyes and let the sensations wash over her. She felt Sam's strong hands lift her slightly as he eased her nightgown past the curve of her hips, his fingertips caressing her bare skin as he drew her firmly towards him.

Chapter 21 - Thursday Afternoon

Jimmy drove the Ford Explorer as Mr G stared pensively at the endless rows of waves marching towards the shore. They'd landed in Westport on time and the keys for the SUV had been waiting for them at the information counter in the terminal as arranged.

As they drove south out of Westport, Mr G felt uneasy. He wasn't comfortable in this rural environment, the emptiness of it. His place was the city, amongst the traffic and the buildings. All he could see here were miles of rocky shoreline on one side, and endless trees and mountains on the other.

He'd dressed as casually as possible, but still felt out of place in his cotton slacks and sports shoes. All the locals seemed to wear were grubby work-pants, frayed bush-shirts and mud-covered gumboots. Any moment now, he expected to see someone sitting on their front porch plucking a banjo.

"How much further to the pub?" Mr G asked Jimmy for the third time.

"According to the GPS, 23 kilometres, we're nearly at Punakaiki."

"Puna fucking what?"

"Punakaiki. You know, where the pancake rocks are. You want to stop for a coffee?"

"No, I just want to get to the pub and see this Ronnie person. The sooner we can get this shit sorted and back to civilisation the better."

Shortly after catching a glimpse of the unusual rock formations off to their right, the Punakaki Cafe came into view. Jimmy slowed to navigate around a tour bus and camper van that had slowed to pull into the car park next to the visitor's centre, but then sped up again as soon as the road was clear.

Fifteen minutes later, Jimmy turned off the highway and pulled up outside the pub.

"What a dump," Mr G said, looking at the rundown building. "I hope they sell a decent brandy."

Jimmy knew it was best just to ignore Mr G when he was in this kind of mood. He jumped out of the car and went around to the passenger side to open the door, only to find Mr G halfway out already.

"Let's get this over with," Mr G said as he marched off towards the door, kicking a pair of gumboots out of his way as he entered. "Bryan said to look out for a guy with bright red hair."

Jimmy followed Mr G as he stormed into the bar. Both men immediately spotted Ronnie pouring a bedraggled looking man with a long grey beard a beer.

"There's our guy," Mr G said.

The two men moved towards an empty space at the bar.

Ronnie had noticed them as they walked through the door. The one in the lead he figured was Mr G. He had a face that looked like it had taken a few punches in its day.

Ronnie finished pouring the beer and made his way to where the two strangers were standing. "You Mr G?"

"Yes, I take it you have some information for me?"

"Let's step into my office," Ronnie said before turning to a staff member and signalling he was going to go out back for a minute.

The three men entered a door at the end of the counter. It led to a moderately sized wood-panelled room containing a desk, filing cabinet, and a couple of straight chairs. Around the walls were historic black and white photos of the village and surrounding area.

While Jimmy looked at the photos, Mr G sized up Ronnie. "So tell me about Sam McKee and how I can find him."

Ronnie could sense why Bryan had mentioned not to piss this guy off. There was something about him that made Ronnie wary, an anger that simmered just below the surface, ready to explode without warning.

Ronnie chose his words well. "Well Sam has been coming down to the West Coast for a few years now, usually rents a cottage somewhere nearby."

"Any idea where?"

"Somewhere further south I think … at least that's the direction he drove off in when he left the pub last time he was here. Where exactly, I don't know."

"So what do you know, exactly?"

"Well I know he's been spending time around Burke Road, a few kilometres south of Punakaki. He usually parks at the end of the road and walks north. There's some good shingle banks with jade in them up that way."

"North from this Burke Road you reckon?"

"Or south … sometimes."

"Well which is it, north or fucking south?"

Had it been anyone other than Mr G asking the question, Ronnie would have said he could only rule out west because unless he was Jesus, he'd drown walking that way, but Mr G didn't look like he had a sense of humour.

"Well it depends on the tides and the weather." Ronnie said. "You just need to follow the footprints below the high tide mark."

"So I'm supposed to be a fucking tracker now?" Mr G shook his head and turned to Jimmy. "You believe this guy?"

"We'll be right Mr G," Jimmy said, flashing a quick look of apology at Ronnie. "I've done some hunting. The footprints should be easy enough to follow."

Mr G turned back to Ronnie at the bar. "Well thanks for the help. You make sure you let me know if Sam turns up. Were staying at The Rocks Motels."

"And the reward?" Ronnie asked sheepishly. "I'll get that when you find him?" Ronnie rummaged through a drawer and grabbed a business card and handed it to Mr G. "In case you need to ring."

Mr G took the card and put it in his pocket. Then he took a step in Ronnie's direction, bringing the two men face to face. "Oh and remember, if you want to stay healthy, we were never here. Got it?"

*****

"Cheeky sod." Lydia laughed squirming in Sam's arms. "Of course it's the first time I've robbed a safe!"

The two of them had been in bed most of the day, getting up only long enough to make some lunch before deciding to return and catch up on some much needed sleep. The problem was, once they got there, sleep was the last thing on their minds.

In between sessions of lovemaking, the two of them talked about their previous lives, their triumphs and regrets, their hopes and desires.

"Right now I'd be happy just for things to get back the way they were," Sam said.

"What about us?" Lydia said pushing herself up so she could see into Sam's eyes. "Is this real or just circumstance?"

"It's likely to be a bit of both. Hey don't get me wrong. In case you hadn't noticed, I'm very attracted to you, but I've also been around long enough to know that relationships formed in unusual situations seem more intense than they do when you're going about your normal lives. Take holiday romances for example."

"Is that what this is?"

Now it was Sam's turn to laugh. "I'd hardly call this a holiday … unless you enjoy having a psychopathic brothel owner trying to kill you."

"It does have its perks though don't you think?" Lydia said, as she swung one leg over Sam and sat up, straddling him. As she stared into Sam's face Lydia started moving slowly back and forth on top of him, leaning forward so her nipples brushed his chest.

"Well at least if I get killed tomorrow I won't die horny."

*****

"You heard the man Jimmy, let's get to this Burke Road and see if we can find that Pajero."

"Sure thing Mr G." Jimmy put the Explorer into gear and accelerated onto the Coast Road. "We've still got a few hours of daylight left."

The only traffic they saw on the drive north was a milk tanker and a couple of campervans heading in the opposite direction. There was no sign of a Pajero down any of the driveways they passed either.

Shortly after passing a big shed, Jimmy saw a side road coming up on their left. He slowed to check the sign. "Yup here we go, Burke Road."

"Okay, stay alert," Mr G said. "We don't want Sam to see us before we see him."

Mr G reached into the glove compartment and pulled out the pistol he'd arranged to be left in the car's glove box when they picked it up. Checking that the safety was on, he released the clip and made sure it was loaded before replacing it and putting the gun back where he'd found it.

When they reached the end of the road there was no sign of a Pajero, just a white truck with a cage on the back. The two men got out of the Explorer, but when they saw a man and a dog walking towards them, Mr G turned around and started heading back to the vehicle.

"Let's go before this guy gets too close a look at us. Last thing we need is to be spotted hanging about," Mr G said. "Let go check out the motel I booked. We can come back here in the morning.

Chapter 22 - Friday Morning

The next morning Sam woke early. After watching Lydia sleep for half an hour or so, he started feeling restless.

"Hey, sleepyhead, wake up." Sam nudged Lydia. "It's a beautiful day, let's go for a walk."

"Huh?" Lydia said, rolling over and pulling the pillow over her head. "I need more sleep."

"Come on, we'll miss the tide if you stay in bed any longer. What say we have a nice walk and then come back for a siesta? You can explain all about these perks again."

"God more sex?" Lydia said with a giggle. "Didn't you get enough yesterday?"

"I got plenty yesterday," Sam said, grinning. "But I'd like plenty today too. I've got a lot of catching up to do."

"Mmmm ... I must say, this hiding out is quite fun."

After having a quick bite to eat, Sam loaded up his daypack with a few snacks and a bottle of water. The weather looked good so he didn't bother packing any rain gear. The high winds of the previous evening had subsided.

"Looks like a T-shirt sort of day, better make it a long sleeved one though, unless you like sand fly bites."

"What are we going to do with the money?" Lydia asked. "It's too risky leaving it here don't you think?"

"Why don't we split the risk? We can hide some here and take the rest with us?"

"Sounds sensible," Lydia said. She started taking the bundles of cash out of her bags and putting them on the table.

While Lydia made two equal stacks, Sam rummaged around the cupboards looking for a container to put them in. On the shelf under the sink, he found a bundle of kitchen-tidy-bags.

"Let's bundle the cash up in these. We can leave half under the cottage, and the rest in the woodshed. The coins are less bulky so we can take those with us. What do you think?"

Lydia nodded in agreement and started packing bundles of notes into the plastic bags. When they had two neat bundles

Sam went around to the back of the cottage and, reaching in as far as he could, pushed one bag under the narrow gap between the cottage's floor and the sandy ground. The black bag was virtually invisible in amongst the shadow.

Next, he went into the wood shed and removed a dozen or so chunks of firewood, before sliding the other bag down with the spiders behind the stack before covering it up again.

"That should do it. Even if someone was looking for the money we'd be incredibly unlucky if they found both bags."

Lydia picked up one of the boxes of coins and tested its weight. It was heavy for its size but still weighed less than a kilogram. "I'll carry one of these in my bag and you can take the other in your backpack."

Sam chuckled at the thought. "Usually I'm hunting for treasure, not taking it with me on my walks," he said as he zipped the velvet box into the pack's front pocket. "This will make a change."

After putting a box of coins in her bag, Lydia hooked her arm through his. "Okay, let's go jade hunting. Find me a nice piece and I'll give you a special treat when we get back."

Sam raised his eyebrows in his best Groucho Marx imitation. "You mean I haven't had the best of you yet?"

Sliding his hand into his pocket he touched his talisman, a lucky piece of jade he always carried with him on a hunt, he could always pretend to find it on their walk if nothing else turned up, but then he figured he'd probably get a treat anyway, especially if the previous day was anything to go by.

"Right fair maiden," Sam said, making a flamboyant sweep of his arm. "Your chariot awaits."

After doing a quick three-point turn, Sam nosed the Pajero out between the flaxes, and pulled onto the main road. After travelling a couple kilometres he pointed off to his right. "They do knife-making classes at that place there. It's great fun from what I've heard. The guy who runs the business is a real character I'm told."

"Sounds like fun."

"They say girls make the best knives. It's probably true too. I saw one that a female backpacker made. God you should have seen it ... more like something a wild Arabian tribesman would carry than a knife some wee Scottish lass had made earlier that day. It looked amazing."

"Girls probably make better knives because all us females have a secret desire to castrate men."

Sam shot a worried look in Lydia's direction, only to find her smirking.

"Ha. Got you!"

"Next door they do jade carving classes," Sam said, trying to ignore Lydia's giggling as she made stabbing motions in his direction. "I wouldn't mind learning to carve one of these days. It would be nice to do something creative with some of the pieces I've found."

As they passed the pub, Sam looked to see if anyone was about, but apart from the backpacker bus, the car park was empty.

"I think this old shed coming up on our left used to be a hanger for a helicopter business, but I don't think it's still going," Sam said, nodding toward the tin-sided building.

Sam didn't mention the white truck with the cage on its back as they passed. Lydia had enough to worry about without alarming her further.

A couple kilometres further on, they turned left onto the gravel of Burke Road.

"Oh look a pukeko," Lydia said.

"They're all over the place around here. I've been told they taste like chicken. Shall I run over one for lunch?"

When Lydia saw Sam's smirk, she punched him playfully on the shoulder. "That's awful. You mean man. They're so cute."

At the end of the road, Sam pulled into his normal parking spot. "It looks like we're first to arrive. That's always a good sign." Sam opened the door of the Pajero and slung his daypack over his shoulder. "I'm glad I packed my gumboots when I came south. If you like, I'll give you a piggyback over the creek, save you getting your feet wet."

"Oh Sir Walter, how gallant," Lydia said, the back of her

hand pressed to her forehead in a melodramatic swoon.

Sam patted his rump. "Come on jump aboard."

Lydia tucked her handbag under her arm and leapt up onto Sam's back. "Giddy up horsey!"

Sam, acting the fool, neighed and pranced his way into the creek, splashing his way to the other side. Once there, he lowered Lydia onto the sand and pointed up the beach to his right. "Let's head north, into the wind. There are some good spots up that way."

As the two of them walked along the high tide mark, Sam did his best to concentrate on looking for jade while keeping up his end of the conversation. Lydia picked up anything colourful.

"Generally jade will be darker than you'd think," Sam said after seeing Lydia pick up a small light green stone. "Sometimes it looks almost black."

"I like the pink ones best." Lydia held out her palm to display a piece of rose quartz. "Look at this one, you can see right through it."

As the sun rose behind them, Sam and Lydia made slow progress down the beach. The surf was pounding in and a dangerous shore break had developed, driven by the strong winds of the previous evening.

"Don't get to close to that surf," Sam said. "That undertow looks nasty."

Sam started to sweat as the temperature rose. When they got to the first major creek, Lydia once again jumped onto his back and got a ride across the shallow stretch of water.

"It feels like you're miles from civilisation out here," Lydia said, spinning around to survey the scene once Sam had put her down again. "Do you run across many people when you're out walking?"

"Sometimes, that's why it pays to be here first. The early hunter gets the jade ... assuming the tide's left us any."

*****

"Slow down Jimmy. That's a Pajero isn't it," Mr G said as they neared the parking area.

"It looks empty. They must be on the beach already," Jimmy said, slowing their vehicle to a crawl and looking around the vicinity.

"Let's get out and see if we can see them."

After pulling in behind a mound of roading gravel left behind by the council, Jimmy got out of the Explorer and started walking towards the beach, scanning the surrounding area for any signs of life.

Mr G reached into the glove box and pulled out the pistol, placing it in the pocket of his windbreaker before following after Jimmy.

"If there's no sign of them we could wait by the car, but I'd rather do what needs doing down on the beach away from prying eyes," Mr G said as he stopped at the edge of the creek. "Fuck, looks like we're going to get wet feet."

After sloshing across the creek, the two men squelched their way towards the thundering surf, looking for Sam and Lydia as they went.

"Here look, footprints." Jimmy said, pointing at a pair of indentations in the sand, one large and one slightly smaller, heading north. "These are recent. See where the tide came up overnight?" Jimmy kicked at a line of disturbed stones and small pieces of driftwood and seaweed. "These prints are well below that."

"Okay but there's no sign of them, they must be further along," Mr G said, looking at the line of prints disappearing into the distance. "If we wait for them beyond that point up there, at least we won't be seen by anyone that happens to come along."

Jimmy nodded and both men started walking. "Yeah we can wait up in the scrub and surprise them when they come back to their car."

*****

"Just up there is where I had my best find ever," Sam said, motioning up the shingle bank towards where he'd found the midden. "I got a patu, a couple of scrapers, two bone needles, and a half-carved tiki all out of the same spot. I never did get around to searching the surrounding area," Sam said. "I seem to recall getting an urgent call from a certain arsehole we both know, wanting me to come back to Wellington before I had the chance."

"Well I'm glad you did, I don't know what I would have done otherwise."

Lydia wrapped her arms around Sam and gave him a kiss.

After Lydia released him, Sam nodded towards the midden. "I don't suppose you feel like having a poke around? Who knows you might just get lucky."

"Sounds like fun big boy, but are you talking jade or something else?"

"God you've got a dirty mind," Sam said with a smirk. "Jade of course."

"Okay, but explain again what I'm looking for?"

"Anything that doesn't look like shingle or toilet paper."

Lydia made a face.

"Let's just work our way methodically around the area I've already excavated," Sam continued. "You never know what we might find."

After scraping a line around the search area with a stout branch, Sam and Lydia got down on their hands and knees and began a careful examination of the site, pulling back the leaves of any plants that obscured their view and removing the top layer of soil. Sam found a few pebbles of interest, mainly quartz and feldspar, but no more artefacts.

They were in the last section of the search grid when a small scrap of knitted fabric poking out of the sand caught Lydia's attention. When she pulled at the fabric, a pair of leggings emerged from the sand.

"Hey look here," Lydia said.

"Are those tights?" Sam asked.

"Yes, but from the pattern on them they don't look very

modern."

Sam made his way over to Lydia for a closer look. "From the fabric's deterioration, I'm guessing these have been buried a few years."

Although the colours were washed out, the stripes on the tights were quite distinctive. From the size of the garment, they looked like something a child or teen would wear.

Sam chucked them towards his daypack and continued searching the area. When a glint of gold caught his eye, he caught his breath.

A short section of chain protruded from the sandy ground. Luckily for Sam, the light had hit the chain just right, causing the briefest of sparkles. When he reached out and pulled on the exposed links, more revealed themselves, along with a couple of animal charms.

The clasp at one end of the chain had broken. Sam wondered if more of the charms may have fallen into the sand when the clasp failed. They looked like solid gold. Maybe the bracelet had come apart without its owner noticing.

"Wow look at this," Sam said holding the bracelet up for Lydia's inspection. "What do you make of this?"

"Nice ... expensive too by the looks of it."

After putting the chain in his shirt pocket, Sam and Lydia dug around a little more, sifting the sand through their fingers.

As he dug deeper, Sam noticed a glint of white.

He brushed some sand away. What he saw looked to be a series of small bones, the remnants of a fish or bird most likely. No more golden charms appeared. As Sam removed more sand around the small bones, a larger bone, about 250mm long appeared. A little more digging and another large bone of a similar size emerged from the ground.

Sam sat back on his haunches for a moment looking at what he'd found. These two bigger bones were too large and too long to be bird bones. Then he realised what they werc.

"Jesus," Sam said. "I'll bet you anything these bones are from a human arm. See," he said pointing at the bones before him, "those little bones are fingers and those two bigger bones are the radius and ulna of the forearm."

Lydia stared, mouth agape, looking down at the bleached pieces lying in the sand. "But—but how the hell did they get here?"

"Well I'll tell you one thing. They're not old enough to be artefacts."

"So what do we do now?"

"We've got to go and report what we've found. A few people have gone missing on the West Coast over the years. This is probably one of them."

*****

Rather than cross another creek, Mr G and Jimmy found a comfortable spot behind a clump of scrub. At least here they were out of sight from the beach, and out of the stiffening wind. While they waited, Mr G pulled out the pistol and practiced sighting down its barrel at a pair of seagulls that had landed near a big pile of seaweed down on the beach.

Every few minutes Jimmy, doing his best meerkat imitation, would poke his head up and look for Sam and Lydia.

"Still no sign of them Mr G."

"Fuck this place," Mr G said, swatting at the sand flies landing on his arms and face. "I'm getting eaten alive."

"Maybe it's the seaweed that's attracting them," Jimmy suggested. "We could move upstream."

"Okay, let try it, anything's got to be better than this."

The two men crouched low as they made their way inland, doing their best to stay out of sight.

Just as they found a new spot Jimmy spotted two dots off in the distance. "Mr G, I think I see people coming."

"It's about fucking time." Mr G had a quick peek before ducking back down behind a small dune covered in grasses. Reaching into his pocket, he pulled out the pistol and handed it to Jimmy. "Here you take this. I prefer to use my friend Mac."

"Mac?" Jimmy said.

"Mac the knife." Mr G said, pulling his trusty blade out of

his pocket. "It's amazing what people are prepared to tell you when Mac is staring them in the face."

Jimmy remembered Ethan. He'd seen the results of Mac's work before.

Five minutes later, Jimmy peeked over the dune again, taking care to stay as low as possible. "It's definitely them. "They're about 300 metres away now. What's the plan boss?"

"Once they've past us, we'll come at them from behind. You keep them covered with the pistol while I have a little chat and persuade them to tell me where my stuff is ... and for fuck sake, if you have to shoot make sure it's in the leg or something. I don't want them dying on me until I get the information I need."

The two men made themselves small, crouching behind the clumps of grass as they waited. After a few minutes, the faint sound of voices carried down the beach on the wind.

When Sam and Lydia passed the spot where Mr G and Jimmy were hiding, they appeared to be in some hurry. "Let's go," Mr G whispered, standing up and moving towards them. Jimmy jumped up and scurried after Mr G who'd already gained five metres on him. When the two men hit the firmer sand below the high tide mark, they both started to jog.

Sam was first to react, spinning around at the scrunch of approaching footsteps.

"Stay right where you are, you thieving motherfucker!" Mr G growled.

Jimmy raised his arm and pointed the pistol in their direction.

Lydia turned and gasped, covering her mouth with one hand and her stomach with the other. "How in the hell ...?"

"Nice to see you again too sweetheart. You thieving cow." Mr G turned briefly towards Jimmy. "If they run, shoot them."

Sam took a step in front of Lydia. "Look we can sort this out. No point in doing something you'll regret later."

"Believe me Sam, I don't have regrets. Only people who steal from me have regrets."

Partially hidden behind Sam's back, Lydia reached into her

handbag and pulled out the box of coins. "Here take them!" Lydia said holding the velvet box out towards Mr G. "You can have your money."

Sam didn't like their chances of survival once Mr G had his valuables back. They were miles from anywhere. What was to stop Mr G from shooting them and burying their bodies on the river flats, just like the one they'd discovered?

"Give me the pistol Jimmy. You go and get the box from Miss Regretful here."

Jimmy handed Mr G the pistol before taking a few cautious steps towards Sam and Lydia.

Sam turned his head slightly and whispered under his breath. "Get ready to run."

When Jimmy reached for the box, Sam grabbed it from Lydia's hand and hurled it towards the surf. Both Mr G and Jimmy turned to follow the box's trajectory as it soared seaward, landing in the wet sand just as a wave retreated.

"Get it Jimmy!" Mr G yelled. "Quickly, before the next wave!"

Jimmy moved fast, but not fast enough. As his fingers wrapped around the box, the next wave crashed onto the shore, sweeping him off his feet, and tossing him over in the surf. As Jimmy regained one knee, the box still in one hand, the wave raced back down the steep beach, dragging Jimmy out with it.

The next wave was a monster. It crashed down on Jimmy with tremendous force, smashing him face first into the churning fist-sized stones before sucking him out again. This time Jimmy didn't get to his feet.

Mr G watched in horror as the shore break tossed Jimmy around like a piece of driftwood, finally dragging him under one last time.

By the time Mr G turned back to Sam and Lydia, they were almost up the shingle bank.

Mr G ran after them letting loose a couple of wild shots. "Stop or I'll kill you, you fucking bastards!"

Sam and Lydia barely heard him. Their arms were pumping

for all they were worth as their toes dug into the loose gravel. Dodging flax bushes, they flew over the top of the bank and raced out onto the flats.

Ten metres further on, Lydia's foot caught on a clump of grass and she hit the ground with a thud.

*****

Just as Mr G crested the shingle bank, a flash of brown came from nowhere. Instinctively he lifted his arm and braced himself for the impact. A clatter of metal sounded as the gun hit the ground moments before his shoulder and hip. The wind burst from his lungs as the dog smashed him down.

After a couple of deep breaths, Mr G twisted his torso in an attempt to get off his back. A wet mountain of fur growled above him. The weight of the animal was surprising. Huge jaws tightened on his forearm as he struggled. Thankful for what little protection the windbreaker gave him against the ivory canines trying their best to rip his arm off, he tried unsuccessfully to push the dog off.

At first Mr G didn't recognise the scream as his own, but as the searing pain raced up his arm, past his shoulder, and beyond, a surge of adrenalin allowed him to find his voice.

"Arrrrgh! Get the fuck off me!"

Mr G's free arm flailed around searching for a weapon, anything that might slow down the animal tearing at his flesh. He latched onto a rock, clutching it in his fist, hoping it would prove his salvation. However, before he could swing the lump of quartz at the dog's massive head, a boot stepped on his wrist, pinning it to the ground.

"I wouldn't recommend hitting Brutus with that rock mister. Not if you want to keep your arm."

Mr G scowled up at the man who was now holding his gun.

"Easy boy," The man in the bush shirt said.

The dog relaxed his grip slightly, following his master's command.

"Get this fucking animal off me!" Mr G yelled.

"All in good time," the man said. "Firstly I want you to let go of that rock."

Sam had stopped to help Lydia up when he heard the commotion behind them. When he turned to see what was going on, Mr G was pinned to the ground by a monstrous German shepherd, one arm firmly between the dog's slathering jaws.

Lydia shivered at the sight and moved closer to Sam, wrapping her arms around his waist from behind.

Mr G moaned and dropped the rock.

"Now when I tell Brutus to release, I want you to roll on your stomach and put your hands behind your back. Believe me mister, you'll be sorry if you don't."

"My fucking arm feels broken you moron."

"Brutus!"

The dog's jaw tightened on Mr G's arm again and a low growl emanated from deep in the dogs chest.

"Okay! I'll do what you say. For fuck sake just get him off me!"

"Brutus heel."

The dog released Mr G's arm and came to sit beside his master. Mr G moaned as he rolled onto his stomach and put his arms behind him.

The man lowered his pack to the ground and pulled a pair of handcuffs from a side pocket. He tucked the pistol into the back of his belt and reached down to fasten the cuffs onto Mr G's wrists before pulling him up into a sitting position.

Sam held Lydia's hand as they walked back towards where Mr G sat on the ground. Blood seeped through the sleeve of Mr G's jacket and a trickle of red ran down his wrist.

Sam nodded towards the stranger. "Hey thanks for helping there, Mr ...?"

"Martin ... Barry Martin. I'm a detective from Christchurch. I must say you two have certainly made this an interesting holiday."

"You're a detective?" Sam asked, wondering how he'd gotten it so wrong.

"Yes. I've come to the West Coast on holiday. I have some unfinished business here on the coast."

"Unfinished business?" Sam said. "What might that be?"

"A cold case early in my career. Nearly fifteen years ago a teenage girl went missing while her family was down here on holiday. I've been looking for her ever since."

"I remember that case," Lydia said. "I was about the same age as the girl that went missing. They found some of her clothing but never found a body."

"That's right," the detective said. "We had a possible sighting of her being driven down Burke Road. A later search of the area found her shoes and a sweatshirt, but her body was never recovered."

"Her poor family," Sam said.

"Not solving the case has driven me crazy. About eight years ago, I joined the dog squad. For my holiday this year I thought I'd come over one more time so Brutus and I could search the area. I know it's a long shot, but for my own sanity I needed to do it."

"Well lucky for us you did." Sam nodded towards Mr G. "This maniac nearly killed us."

"I noticed," the detective said. "I caught sight of you as Brutus and I were rounding the point. I could see the man was armed so I couldn't afford to rush right in. We had to get near enough for Brutus to have a chance of reaching him before he could get off a shot. Sorry for leaving it to the last moment."

"No need to apologise, I'm just pleased you were here," Sam said.

As he spoke to Detective Martin, Sam eased closer to where Mr G was sitting with his hands behind his back. Holding the eye of the detective, Sam took one final step forward and brought the toe of his gumboot down on Mr G's hands. With downward pressure and a sharp twist, Sam ground Mr G's fingers into the ground."

"Owww fuck! Watch it moron. You're standing on my fucking hand!"

Sam's eyes sparkled as he turned towards Lydia and smiled,

before looking down at Mr G.

"Oops sorry Mr G, I didn't realise."

With all his weight on Mr G's hand, he gave his toe one last twist, before stepping back and putting his arm around Lydia's waist, drawing her towards him.

By the time Mr G was raised to his feet, his pockets searched, the knife in his possession confiscated, and they'd all reassembled on the beach, there was no sign of Jimmy.

"Looks like your friend didn't make it," Detective Martin said. "This beach is treacherous when it's breaking close to shore like this."

"Speaking of which," Sam said, "we'd better get moving, tides coming in."

Sam and Lydia walked beside the detective as he led Mr G down the beach.

The detective's comments made Sam curious. "So you've been thinking about this missing girl all this time? Sorry, but when I saw you wandering around the flats, I was beginning to think you were a nut job."

The Detective Martin laughed softly. "I was suspicious of you too. Everywhere I went you seemed to turn up. Why did you stop your truck by the house I rented?"

"You saw me?"

"I was out at the shed, getting wood for the fire and saw you sneaking around."

Sam looked down at his feet. "Just being nosey I guess. Wondering why you were digging graves out on the flats."

"That wasn't a grave. Jesus … I was investigating a depression that might have been a burial site. Brutus got a bit excited you see. Unfortunately it turned out to be sheep bones."

"So I'm assuming you didn't take any pot shots at me either?"

"Pot shots? Why in God's name would I do that?"

"Do you get shot at often?" Lydia asked, hearing this news for the first time. "Maybe being around you is more dangerous than you're letting on."

"You can talk," Sam said, grinning at Lydia before turning

back to the detective. "And the note under my wiper blades?"

"I was hoping to find the girl and some evidence linked to whoever killed her without any of the locals knowing what I was up to. If the killer still lives in the area, and finds out what I'm doing, they might move the body to another location and then I'll never find her. You were just a little too nosey for my liking."

"Why so keen to find the girl?"

"That's a long story, but the short version is that my daughter died a few years back … leukaemia. Burying her was the toughest thing I ever did. But despite that, at least I had someone to bury. I had some closure. The parents of this girl never got that."

"Well there's a chance Lydia and I may be able help you solve your mystery."

"How's that?"

Sam reached into his top pocket and pulled out the charm bracelet, passing it to the detective.

"We found this and what looks like human bones down near the second creek when we were fossicking for artefacts. We were just heading back to report our find when Mr G jumped us."

"And you can take me there?"

Sam nodded. "Seeing you just saved our lives, I reckon it's the very least I can do."

Chapter 23 - Friday Morning

As promised, Sam and Lydia met Detective Martin at the end of Burke Road early the next morning. Detective Martin had asked them not to tell a soul about finding the bones until he'd had a chance to check the find out for himself.

"I appreciate you doing this for me," Detective Martin said. "I've spent so much time on this case. It's hard to believe it might be coming to an end."

A number of police and emergency services crews had come to the scene to search for Jimmy's body. Sam could see a pair of quad bikes being unloaded from a trailer, while two men in wetsuits stood watching.

When Brutus was let out of his cage, he romped up to Sam and nuzzled his hand in greeting. Lydia got down on one knee and scratched Brutus behind the ears, getting a series of licks in return.

"He likes you," the Detective Martin said. "He's a great police dog, but sometimes I think he'd prefer to slobber people to death rather than bite them."

"I bet he would," Lydia said giving Brutus another scratch. "Who's a good boy!"

"So how did you go with Mr G in Greymouth?" Sam asked the detective.

"No problem at all. After my sworn statement he was charged with attempted murder. Forensics has taken Mr Graham's gun and knife away for analysis. If he's used either of them in the commission of a crime they'll soon know about it."

"Well the longer he's in jail the better as far as I'm concerned," Sam said.

"That's for sure," Lydia agreed.

"That diary and CD you gave us should open up a few avenues of investigation. As you know, blackmail and corruption are serious offences."

While Detective Martin went to speak with one of his

colleagues, Sam took Lydia's hand and pulled her aside. "It doesn't sound like Mr G has mentioned the cash and the coins."

"Maybe he's afraid of getting tax evasion and money laundering added to the list of charges?"

Detective Martin said something to one of the men near the quad bikes, pointing in the direction of where Jimmy had gone missing before coming back over to join Sam and Lydia.

"Sorry about that. I was just trying to explain to the searcher how the currents work around here. I did some study on them when we thought the girl's killer might have dumped her body into the sea."

"Well Detective," Sam said, "shall we take a walk so I can show you where we found these bones?"

The detective hesitated a moment at the prospect of finally realising a goal he'd had for so long. He turned away from Sam and pulled a handkerchief out of his pocket.

Sam looked out to sea to give the man some time to get his emotions in check. There was no rush. It was a lovely day, the waves had died down, and the wind was barely perceptible. In fact, on a day like this, and with Lydia by his side, Sam couldn't think of a better place to be.

Finally the detective spoke. "Yes I'd like that very much."

As they walked three abreast along the beach, the detective reached into his pocket and pulled out a photograph. "You know, I've carried this for fifteen years. I look at it every day."

Sam took a quick look at the photo, and suddenly realised why the detective had been staring at the young girl in the pub the other day. The two girls could have been twins.

While they walked and talked, Brutus ran up the shingle bank, smelling things and peeing on everything possible, thoroughly enjoying himself.

As they neared the site of the midden, Sam slowed and pointed inland. "The bones are just up there."

"Heel Brutus!" Detective Martin yelled, calling the dog so he wouldn't disturb any potential evidence. "Good boy, come here."

Brutus ran up and stood by his master, his tongue hanging loose and tail wagging.

"Sit Brutus," the detective said, giving the dog a pat. "Stay here boy."

As Brutus sat waiting for his next command, Sam led the way up towards the collapsed bank.

"As soon as we realised the bones were human we stopped digging," Sam said, walking towards a slight depression in the earth just beyond the midden. He raised his arm and pointed. "It's just there."

Detective Martin bent down on one knee and examined the site. He crouched there for a full minute, staring at the shards of white before reaching into his pocket and pulling out a pair of latex gloves.

From another pocket, he removed a small paintbrush, which he used to loosen the soil from around the finger bones. As he brushed, more bones appeared. The three fingers that Sam had uncovered, were now five, each consisting of multiple segments.

"These are human bones alright. By the size of them they look about right to be my missing girl."

Then for some reason, Detective Martin took a sharp intake of breath and stopped brushing. He pulled a plastic bag and a pair of tweezers from his inside pocket.

"What do you see?" Sam asked as he moved a little closer.

Leaning forward, the detective reached down with the tweezers and carefully pulled at what looked to be a small tuft of matted fabric wrapped around two of the finger bones. He dropped the evidence into the plastic bag and zip-locked it together.

As the detective stood and held the bag up towards the light for a closer view, Sam stepped forward to see what it was the detective had discovered. This time it was Sam's turn to gasp.

There in the bag, without any doubt, and as clear as clear could be, was a clump of incredibly bright red hair.

Sam and the detective looked at each other, and then spoke in unison.

"Ronnie!"

Sam couldn't believe what he was seeing. "It must have been Ronnie that took those pot shots at me the other day, trying to scare me off the beach in case I stumbled across evidence of his crime. The bugger tried to convince me it was rabbit shooters!"

Chapter 24 - Saturday Morning

The next morning, Sam and Lydia woke up to another brilliant day on the West Coast. The sun had just risen over the Alps and was angling through the window and into the cottage where they lay curled up on the bed.

"What do you think will happen to Ronnie?" Lydia asked.

Sam rolled over onto one elbow, and gently brushed Lydia's long hair off her face. "When I spoke to Detective Martin after Ronnie's arrest yesterday, he said that with the new DNA evidence the case against Ronnie should be a slam dunk."

"I wonder why he did it."

"Who knows," Sam said. "Maybe the hard time he got as a child affected him more than people realised. I doubt we'll ever know the whole story. He seemed so normal. Who would have guessed?"

"I can't stop thinking about the poor girl, out there on the beach, scared and alone."

Sam stroked Lydia's cheek. "At least she was a fighter, grabbing that handful of hair should bring her killer to justice."

Lydia shook her head, as if to rid herself of evil thoughts. "So what would you like to do today?"

Sam shrugged. "Do you want to head back to Wellington, or would you rather stay around here for a few more days? I've got the place booked for another week you know."

"Let's spend the week here," Lydia said. "You can show me all your favourite places. Then next week we can go and spend some time in my favourite spot. Sound fair?"

Sam smiled at Lydia. "Hmmm ... sounds like a plan."

"Great." Lydia beamed at Sam and planted a big kiss on his lips.

"So where is this favourite place of yours?"

"I want to go back to Paris. Now, thanks to Mr G's cash, I can."

"Paris ... of course," Sam said, remembering the photo of Lydia smiling in front of the Eiffel tower and the travel brochure Mr G had given him when starting his search. "Hey, can we do some day trips out into the countryside while we're there?"

"Sure. What did you have in mind?"

"Well I read an article a few weeks back about someone finding a fossilised mammoth about 50k east of Paris. Maybe we could go and have a poke around? Who knows we might get lucky."

Lydia swung one leg over Sam and straddled him. She leaned forward until her breasts pressed against his chest and her lips were close to his. With one hand she reached around and guided him into her.

"No need to go to Paris for that Sir Galahad. I think you're about to get lucky right now."

*****

ALSO BY BLAIR POLLY

Bad Chillies

When eight-year-old Leonard Bourne is abducted, his parents pay a huge ransom, following the kidnapper's instructions to the letter. But instead of getting their son back, they receive a chilli jar containing one of his fingers and a note demanding more money.

Realising their mistake, they do what they should have done in the first place, they call the police.

Wellington detectives Chris Spacey and Andy Thompson get lucky and catch the sadistic kidnapper, but after the kidnapper escapes from prison, two more children disappear, and a desperate hunt begins. Will police find the children before they are brutalised? Or will someone take the law into their own hands?

Set in Wellington, New Zealand, over a period of one gruelling week, *Bad Chillies* tells a story about a darker side of human nature. It also illustrates how some parents don't know their children quite as well as they think they do.

"A fast-paced crime thriller with a chilling ending you won't expect."

ALSO BY BLAIR POLLY

Art, Shark, and a Coffin Named Denzel

Art, Shark, and a Coffin Named Denzel is a suspenseful and emotional roller-coaster that will have you laughing one moment and crying the next.

Alex is a sculptor with big dreams and an over-active imagination. When he hooks up with the gorgeous Lisa, he can't believe his luck, but Lisa has a secret that threatens not only her budding relationship with Alex, but the lives of Alex's friends as well.

Art, Shark, and a Coffin Named Denzel is a humorous insight into the workings of a creative mind. It is a story about friendship, love, courage, and how valuable time becomes, when it's about to run out.

"A quirky, suspenseful, and funny read."

* * *

You can email Blair Polly at: bpolly@xtra.co.nz
Or view his website: www.blairpolly.com

CPSIA information can be obtained at www.ICGtesting.com
Printed in the USA
LVOW062007040713

341429LV00001B/271/P